The Elephant in the Dark

The Elephant in the Dark

by CAROL CARRICK

pictures by DONALD CARRICK

Clarion Books

TICKNOR & FIELDS : A HOUGHTON MIFFLIN COMPANY

New York

Acknowledgment

With grateful thanks to General Curator Mike Crocker and the elephant handlers of the
Dickerson Park Zoo in Springfield, Missouri, for sharing their knowledge
of elephants with me.

Clarion Books
Ticknor & Fields, a Houghton Mifflin Company
Text copyright © 1988 by Carol Carrick
Illustrations copyright © 1988 by Donald Carrick

Library of Congress Cataloging-in-Publication Data
Carrick, Carol.
The elephant in the dark / Carol Carrick : illustrations by Donald Carrick.
p.   cm.
Summary: Through training an elephant, the first ever seen in 1830's Massachusetts,
orphan Will begins to feel important for the first time in his life.
ISBN 0-89919-757-4 : $12.95 (est.)
[1. Elephants — Fiction. 2. Orphans — Fiction. 3. Massachusetts —
Fiction.] I. Carrick, Donald, ill. II. Title.
PZ7.C2344El 1988
[Fic] — dc19   88-2591   CIP   AC
A   10 9 8 7 6 5 4 3 2 1

To D.F.C., with love

Also by Carol Carrick
Illustrated by Donald Carrick

Stay Away from Simon!
What a Wimp!
Some Friend!

Contents

I

Teased at School

When Will was little, he and his mother used to snuggle in bed on a cold morning as if nothing else in the world needed doing. While she told him stories about spirits that dwelled in the trees, Will thought he could see them in the shadows on the ceiling. But now he was twelve and had to be at school.

School. Will rolled over and pulled the covers tighter around his head. Hoofs tapped restlessly in the kitchen below and on the other side of the curtain, his mother was coughing. With a groan, Will threw off the covers and stepped into his trousers, hopping as his feet hit the icy floor.

"Shoo!" He climbed down from the bedroom loft, nudging the hens off the ladder. Each morning his mother was charmed to find a brown egg left on a chair seat, or tucked behind the fireside broom. They ate the eggs and milked Butternut, the goat, but Will didn't know till he started school that other families kept their chickens for food. Walter Keeler had brought a chicken leg in his lunch pail one day.

"Eat my darlings?" Maddy, his mother, had shuddered when Will told her about Walter.

"My pretty girl," she said, stroking Sukey's feathers. "How could I do such a thing!"

Maddy called all of the chickens by name. She even wrote poems about them. In the woods behind the house, there were graves with little wooden markers. One said Birdie on it, one said Lovey, and another Henny Mae.

Will bridled at the sniggers when he heard his mother called the "chicken lady." Didn't other people make fools over themselves with their cats and dogs, feeding them with scraps from their own table? Cap'n Riggs, his teacher, even kept a crow, a noisy, bad-tempered bird that nipped people.

Both of the feed sacks were empty, so Will let the goat and the chickens out to forage. All he found for himself were the beans left from supper. He bolted them down and called good-bye to his mother. He was going to be late again.

Out on the road Will was sorry he hadn't worn his winter shirt. It was cold for September and the one he wore wasn't enough to keep him warm. Even though the school bell was already ringing, he ducked between Sanderson's fence rails and picked up a few windfall apples.

He'd be fiercely hungry by lunchtime. Then he started to run. Cap'n Riggs was strict about being on time.

Will ran past Sanderson's. In the early 1800s, the village of Cadbury, Massachusetts, had a Congregational church, a school, and Sanderson's General Store. Three old-timers and one of the local dogs were sunning themselves on the porch. They all took an interest in Will as he passed.

The dog, a scrappy little mongrel, came every day for a handout from Mrs. Sanderson. Will steeled himself as it rushed at him barking. It was a daily ritual for them.

"Go get 'em, Snuff," one of the men called in his reedy voice, and the other two slapped their knees and cackled at the humor of this.

Will's heart pounded. Somehow dogs always barked at him. One had even bitten his hand when he held it out to make friends. So far, Snuff had only barked. But Will could never be sure. Just as he thought Snuff had given up and gone back to the porch, the dog gave one last bark close behind Will's heels. To his disgrace, Will flinched.

"Better hurry, boy," one of the men called from the porch. "Yer gonna be late."

Will stuffed down his anger and in spite of the schoolmaster's temper, slowed stubbornly to a walk. When the men were out of sight, he broke into a run again, past the church and across Tea Lane. Luckily, the children were still filing in when he reached the schoolyard.

There was an empty place left on a bench in the second

row. Just as Will got there, Peter Beers, the miller's son, slid sideways to fill it. He was a large boy with small, piggy eyes and the suggestion of a mustache along his upper lip.

"Let me sit down," Will said.

"There ain't no room," answered Peter. The mustache spread in a satisfied grin.

Will tried to slip into the space on the other side of Peter, but the boy shifted back again, filling it.

"Move over." Will scowled, annoyed by the teasing.

Cap'n Riggs rapped his stick on the desk, the signal for the class to come to order. By this time, the boys on either side of Peter had caught on to the game and began to close all the spaces.

Will was left with no place to sit. "Come on," he whispered more urgently. Peter was going to get him in trouble.

"Will Sleeper," the retired sea captain boomed in his voice of command. "Take your seat."

"They won't let me."

Cap'n Riggs pointed to the far end of the row.

Will moved to the space, tripping over the bigger boys' feet. His ears burned with embarrassment.

Under the fierce gaze of the Captain, forty pupils from the age of four to seventeen grew still. Willing, or unwilling, they would spell out words and add up columns of numbers by copying what the Captain wrote in chalk on the painted wall behind his desk. Few of them owned any kind of book.

The morning began with reading. As the teacher's Bible was passed down Will's row, each boy read haltingly from the book of Joshua, stumbling over the difficult words. Will loved stories. When it was his turn, he stood up and read with fascination how the children of Israel had made a great shout on the seventh day and the walls of Jericho had fallen.

"Very good," Riggs interrupted. "Next." Will sat down, feeling the triumph of Joshua until he saw Peter's sneer.

Just before recess, a ripple of whispers moved down the row of boys, starting with Peter. Will grew anxious as he realized they were plotting something. Then the boys fixed their eyes on the teacher's face until he said they were free to leave. At Peter's signal, they all rose at once except Will on the end. Peter's end of the crude bench rose, like a dory cresting a wave, and Will toppled over with a crash.

Everyone on the other benches turned around. The little ones looked startled until Peter shook his head at Will.

"Clumsy," he said. Then they all understood it was a joke and began to giggle.

Will stuffed down his rage and struggled to pick up the heavy bench. Then, careful not to catch anyone's eye, he pushed his way out of the room past Cap'n Riggs who frowned as though it was Will who had caused the disturbance.

The pupils rushed out to claim their favorite spots in the sunny yard. Will climbed a tree that shaded the corner and watched hungrily as the others spread out their lunches;

homemade sausages and bread, applesauce and cold pie. The bigger girls sat in a sociable huddle. A few of them strung the rose hips they had picked on the way to school, making necklaces for their dearest friends.

Hidden by the thick branches of the oak tree, Will ate his apples and watched a game of I Spy. Even the littlest boys were included. He wished he could climb down and join them but he didn't know how. Why was he always the butt of their teasing?

The rest of the school day passed slowly. The sun moved around to Will's side, overheating the classroom, and the chanting of the little ones put him in a trance. Dreaming of Joshua's victory over his enemies, Will saw himself as the leader of his people. At his command they gave a great shout and the walls around Jericho fell once again.

After school Will and his mother searched the trees for wild grapevines to make into baskets. The late afternoon was golden. Drowsy bees hovered in the asters along the roadside.

"We have enough vines, don't you think?" Will said anxiously as a spasm of coughing shook Maddy. "If you need more I can fetch them." For as long as Will could remember, his mother had had the cough, but it was getting worse.

On the way home, his mother laid a hand on his arm to slow him down. Will frowned with concern. He wasn't walking that fast.

Maddy tried to reassure him. "It's just those long legs of

yours," she teased, "I can't keep up." She knew he was proud of being almost her height. That was what Will loved about his mother; she made him feel good about things. He almost told her about Peter and school, how unhappy he was. But she wouldn't understand his feelings about being different. Maddy didn't want to fit in.

A chipmunk swung from the the end of an elderberry branch, stuffing berries into its fat cheeks. "Just look at the dear little thing." Maddy laughed but then her breath was caught by another fit of coughing.

Will's mother had cut a worn-out petticoat into handkerchiefs. She took out one of these scraps and coughed into it. Then she quickly stuffed it back into her pocket, but not before Will had seen the bloody flecks of mucus on it. Because his mother tried to hide her sickness, it was all the more frightening to him.

II

Earning Money

The next day, Will stopped at the general store after school. Children with a penny to spend there could buy candy. Will thought wistfully about what a penny could buy . . . lemon drops or a peppermint stick. Even though Will didn't have a penny, he had a reason to go in there today. He needed feed for the animals.

Peter Beers blocked the door. "Goin' clammin'?" he asked, looking at Will's bare feet and the trousers that left off above his ankles.

Backing up Peter was a new boy the others called Wood Tick. He was a skinny boy with hair hanging in his eyes. Wood Tick had been friends with Will at first until he started hanging around with Peter.

"Aaaah." Peter stuck his tongue out. It was flaming red, and on the tip perched the remains of a hot cinnamon drop.

Wood Tick did the same, but his fell off.

"Fool!" Peter shoved him and the two of them scuffled until Peter stepped on the candy.

Will pretended to ignore them, but squeezing past he caught the spicy smell of cinnamon on their breath.

Once inside the store, his eyes wandered lovingly over its wealth: dried fruit and crackers, pickled fish and beef, kettles, harness, nails, and bone-handled knives. His eyes rested longest on the sugared doughnuts.

Mrs. Sanderson was leaning on the counter, squinting at the New Bedford paper. "When are you bringing me some baskets?" she asked Will without looking up.

"Soon, I guess," he mumbled. From the time his dark head could barely reach the counter, Will had been bringing in his mother's grapevine baskets to sell. But this year she hadn't started on them.

Will lifted a sack of feed and hefted it over his shoulder. "I see your apples are dropping." He hesitated before he spoke, but the sack was heavy. "If I picked them, could I work off the cost of this feed?"

Mrs. Sanderson sighed. From the way the boy looked, she suspected he never got a decent meal. He would probably eat half of what he picked.

Will licked his chapped lips while she considered. "Wait much longer and they'll all be wormy," he said.

Lottie Sanderson glanced out the window. It was true her apples lay thick on the ground, buzzing with wasps. Leon, the hired man, was too stiff for tree climbing, and the apples that fell were bruised and wouldn't keep anyway.

At last Lottie gave in. "All right," she said, straightening her shoulders, "but you get the feed *after* you pick the apples." Her husband was too soft about giving credit. Half of Cadbury owed him money.

"Yes'm," Will said with relief. He eased down the bag of feed. Butternut could forage for a few days more.

"Better go out back and tell Mr. Sanderson," the woman said, returning to her paper.

Will hurried toward the door to the back room.

Mrs. Sanderson frowned. "Just a minute." She reached for a doughnut. "This ain't gonna sell no more today. Why don't you eat it so's I can wash the tray."

Will snatched the doughnut and bolted it down. Then he remembered his manners. "Thank you, M'am," he started to say, but a crumb stuck in his windpipe.

Mr. Sanderson was sitting on a barrel in the storeroom, trading stories with two of the local farmers. One of them, Elmer Athearn, left off slicing a chew from his plug of tobacco. "Feather in your throat?" he asked as Will came in, choking.

Will struggled to speak, his eyes streaming with tears. He gave a few coughs. "Mrs. Sanderson says for me to pick apples," he said at last.

The storekeeper rubbed the few hairs that covered the shine on his head. "Sure," he said amiably. "Why not. Come around tomorrow. You can use those." He nodded toward a pile of sacks in the corner.

"Yessir." Will backed away, wiping his hands nervously

on his trousers. He turned and left, feeling the farmers' eyes between his shoulders. He couldn't wait to tell his mother he had a job.

On the road home, James Norton passed with a wagon-load of seaweed. The pungent, salty smell made Will think of when he and Maddy lived with Grandfather.

Grandfather had been a fisherman. Will could barely remember standing on the beach, hiding in the shelter of his mother's skirts while Grandfather and the other men hauled in their boats. After Grandfather was lost at sea, Will and his mother moved inland to the little house on Tiah's Cove Road. It was just a shed with a loft, really, and a ramshackle chicken house out back.

Once, when he was little, Will asked his mother why he didn't have a father like other children. Maddy hugged him. She loved him more than any child was ever loved, she had said, and he belonged to her alone. He didn't need a father.

Her words had given him comfort, but Will still wished for a father. Later, he learned his father had been a fisherman, too. When Will asked whether his father had also been lost at sea, his mother said no, he had left before Will was born.

When Will reached the Norton place the farmer was working with his oldest son, banking seaweed against the foundation of their house to keep out the winter cold. Will watched the two of them work silently together, the man and his boy, and then he walked on.

Dragging his feet in the dust, Will pretended how one day his father would return. He would have dark hair and eyes like Will, and they would know each other at once. A noisy flock of chickadees startled him out of his daydream. They dropped through the maple leaves overhead like the spatter of rain. A sure sign of fall.

Maddy sat in the doorway, her face lifted to the warmth of the sun, her red hair blazing in the light. Will tried to sneak up and surprise her but she opened her eyes. "I've been waiting for you," she told him.

Will burst out with his news. "I've got a job picking apples," he said, sitting down next to his mother. "Tomorrow. At Sanderson's."

"The trees are so lovely with their apples," she said dreamily. "It's sad how they drop off."

Will was startled sometimes by the way his mother reacted to things. This time he was disappointed. He had thought she'd be pleased that he had gotten work. Even the goat and the chickens couldn't live off the land now that winter was coming. If all of them were to eat, they would need money. Wasn't she worried about that?

*

That Saturday, Will stood on a ladder and picked apples till his ankles ached. In midafternoon, Leon, the handyman, brought a wagon full of boxes. Carefully he and Will packed only the perfect fruit in sawdust. Leon looked disagreeable, as though the boy was putting him to a good deal of trouble. It took the pleasure out of the work for

Will. The old man's hands shook as they bent over the boxes, and his breath had a winy, sour smell like the crushed apples.

They carted the boxes of good apples back to the store where Will carried them down to the root cellar. Then he and Leon heaped the bruised fruit and windfalls next to the cider press. After they finished, Sanderson told the boy he might take all the apples he could carry. Will filled two sacks so full that on the way home, he had to stop every few yards to rest.

That night he and his mother sat peeling and coring apples in their kitchen. Maddy sang the sea chanteys she had learned as a girl while they sliced the apples and strung them to dry in front of the chimney. When they were done they fed the great pile of peelings to Butternut and the chickens. The heat of the fire soothed Will's aches, and the apples hanging like holiday festoons gave him a satisfied feeling.

Last fall and winter they had sat like this while his mother wove baskets, beautiful ones in every size and shape: egg baskets, apple baskets, baskets in melon shapes dyed in many colors. Will frowned at the heap of vines they had picked last week. His mother hadn't touched them at all.

Maddy's eyes followed his gaze to the vines in the corner. Her damp skin gleamed like candle wax in the light of the fire, and there were unnatural spots of color in her

cheeks. Will felt a flutter of panic in his chest. Who would take care of them if his mother didn't get well? If only he could find his father.

Feeling the need to do something, Will shoved a new log in the fireplace, nearly putting out the flame. He thought with bitterness of the man who had fathered him. A real father would be here to look after them now, but his father hadn't even waited for his birth.

The room darkened and wisps of smoke drifted out from between the logs. Maddy began to cough. Sometimes her cough made Will angry, as if she could stop if she only tried. He jumped to his feet and stabbed at the logs until flames burst from the bark and sparks shot up the chimney.

III

Maddy

Blue sky lit the puddles on Will's way home from school. It had rained most of the week, drumming steadily overhead while the children recited their lessons, and keeping them in during recess. So that Thursday, when the sun finally appeared, it raised everyone's spirits.

A frog stared glassily at Will, its throat throbbing a pearly bubble of skin. Up ahead, Wood Tick let out a shriek as Peter stomped in a puddle. They hadn't bothered Will any since last week. Still, he dawdled on the road to avoid catching up with them.

The usual loafers ranged the length of Sanderson's porch. Something across the road had captured their attention and Peter and his friends stopped to see what it was. As Will came along they started snickering.

Will knew they were waiting for him and he took a deep breath to ready himself for their meanness. He would walk by as quickly as he could.

"O Godfrey!" he groaned, looking over in Athearn's pasture. It was his mother. She was out there on her knees, wearing only her night clothes. Had she gone crazy?

He scrambled over the wall.

"Will!" Maddy sat back on her heels and smiled up at him. Next to her was a basket of mushrooms.

"Mother," he hissed. "What are you doin'?"

The wet grass had soaked his mother's undergarment with dew, and to Will's embarrassment, he could see the form of her body through the wet cloth.

He looked away, angrily. "You oughten' to show yourself like that," he said.

Maddy clutched the hem of his trousers. "Will . . . look," she said, pointing out the circle of mushrooms that had sprung up in the grass. "A fairy ring!" Her eyes shone with excitement.

Will didn't care about the mushrooms. He was too painfully aware of the small crowd watching them. "Please, Mother," he begged, with a glance toward the general store. "Come home with me."

Just then Lottie Sanderson hustled out on the porch. "You people got nothin' better to do?" she scolded the men. "Making fun of that poor creature." She pushed through them down the steps, flapping her apron as if they were a flock of geese.

The gawkers got ready to watch the fun. All except George Peebles, that is. George had come into the store with a basket of late spinach, so anxious to spread the news about Maddy that he forgot to tie his horse. "Whoa, Betsy!" he called, running down the street. His cart disappeared around the corner as old Betsy plodded home.

Mrs. Sanderson hobbled across the street and through the gate of Athearn's pasture. With her skirts raised above the wet grass, she picked her way over to Will's mother. Seeing the young woman's flushed face, she said, "Your mother has a fever, Will. It's gotten her a little confused."

Will gave Mrs. Sanderson a grateful look.

"Here," Lottie said gruffly, bending over his mother. "Come along with me, Maddy. I'll take you home."

But Maddy ignored her. "Look at all of 'em!" She spread her arms to embrace the whole pasture, its green velvet dotted with white buttons. "Aren't they lovely?"

By this time a cluster of school children had joined Peter. Will sighed his impatience. Why did Maddy have to do this? He wanted to shake his mother. Of course folks made fun of her when she acted so crazy.

Lottie nodded at the mushrooms. "They're real nice. Now give me your arm, dear, and we'll go home."

Maddy smiled and tossed her head as if she would resist. But when Lottie hauled her to her feet she gave in like a docile child.

Mrs. Sanderson took off her apron and covered his mother's bare shoulders. "You bring the basket," she told Will.

The children stepped back as his mother was brought

through the gate. Will trailed behind the two women, wishing he was invisible. He hung his head, feeling disgraced, and refused to look at anyone.

Will was relieved when they got as far as the bend at Brandy Brow. The ruins of the old inn would hide them from sight, but it wasn't till they came to Norton's farm that he found the courage to look over his shoulder. A small knot of children were still watching from the bend.

Will lagged behind the women, not wanting to talk to them. The walk had worsened his mother's cough and slowed them down. He was shocked by how thin Maddy was, repelled by her body. Her bare arm was no more than a bone.

At last they reached home. Exhausted now, Maddy sank down in one of the chairs. Mrs. Sanderson drew up the other one to sit herself, but saw that the chickens had whitened it with their droppings. She leaned on the table instead. Uncomfortable with her there, Will stood in the doorway.

Mrs. Sanderson fished out a handkerchief from her sleeve. While she blotted her face and throat, her eyes traveled to the delicate drawings pinned to the walls. "Pretty," she commented.

"Mother made them." Will said it sullenly, but looking at the pictures, he remembered the summer evenings Maddy had filled by scratching the wildflowers and animals on birch bark.

Will wished that Mrs. Sanderson would leave. She wasn't unkind, but somehow her being there spoiled the things that he'd liked. Now, even his shell collection looked faded, and the spotted birds' eggs dusty. He saw the room as it must look to her . . . the spiders' webs Maddy would not disturb, the drifts of goat hair, the dusty windowpanes. Last winter he had stuffed rags in the holes, but the way they looked had never bothered him before. Nobody ever came to their house.

Maddy rocked in the straight chair, hugging her arms. "Maybe she should be in bed," Mrs. Sanderson said to Will. She went over and took his mother's hand. "You should be in bed, Maddy." She said it again even louder, "Shall we put you to bed?"

When his mother didn't answer, Lottie looked around to see where she slept. Will pointed to the loft. "Up there," he said.

Mrs. Sanderson seemed nervous about the ladder. "Can the two of you manage?" she asked.

Will nodded. He helped Maddy up the ladder and into bed. Seeing how dazed she was, he felt ashamed that he'd been so angry with her. When he came down he was relieved when Mrs. Sanderson said, "I should get back to the store. You mind, now, it's best if your mother keeps to home."

Will was happy to be left alone. His stomach growled; it seemed as if he was always hungry. He checked the cupboard for something to eat, knowing there would be nothing but apples. He'd eaten too many the last few days and his innards were upset. He had needed to visit the privy so often that there were snickers every time he left the schoolroom.

Will saw the basket of mushrooms on the table. He poked at the firm white buttons with distaste. Since there was nothing else for dinner, he stirred up the fire and sliced them in the pan to fry. Cooked with a flour gravy, they would fill his stomach, but the slippery mess put him in mind of the slugs he killed in the garden.

First he brought some of the mushrooms up to his mother, but she said she wasn't hungry. Instead, she took his hand and squeezed it, looking into his face. Will lowered his eyes from hers. He wanted to ask if she was going to get well, but he was afraid that maybe she wasn't.

Downstairs, Biddy, the speckled hen, was pecking at the firewood. Now and then she found a wood louse that had come in with the logs.

"The feed," Will remembered, smacking his forehead. He'd meant to pick it up today; the weather had been too wet before this. To punish himself for being angry with his mother, he would go back for it now. By then it would almost be time to milk Butternut. Then he could fix his mother some hot milk with a little wild honey in it to soothe her cough. He wanted to do something for her.

*

Sanderson was prying the lid from a barrel of oatmeal when Will came for the grain he'd been promised. "You earned that, son," the man said, stopping to rest on his crowbar.

Will mumbled a thank you, keeping his eyes on the floor. There was a spot there and he rubbed it with his big toe.

Lottie Sanderson gave her husband a look full of meaning. Like most folks in Cadbury, she didn't think much of Maddy Sleeper and her strange ways but she felt sorry for the boy.

The storekeeper cleared his throat. "Could use a good worker," he said. "How 'bout coming in mornings, before school?"

"Sure!" Will's face brightened.

Sanderson gave Will a key to open up the store. On the way home whenever he stopped to shift the feed sack to his other shoulder, Will took out the key to make sure he hadn't lost it. He'd never had a key in his possession before.

IV

A Monster in the Barn

For the past two weeks, Will had looked forward every day to that first pungent smell of hemp, molasses, cheese, and tobacco as he opened up the store. He had a reason to come there now, and he was getting paid for it.

But this morning Will's shoulders felt stiff and his eyes burned from lack of sleep. Mother had tossed with fever during the night, and he had lain awake, afraid to shut his eyes until she was quiet again. When he arrived at the store, he saw that he was late: The shutters were already down and the door was open for business.

He hurried around back to feed the horse. Just his luck, Sanderson was standing in front of the barn with someone, a stranger wearing city clothes. They both stopped talking when they saw Will.

"Got somethin' inside for ya," Sanderson said, and the two men looked amused.

Will winced. He knew he wasn't going to like this.

Somehow they were planning to make fun of him like the kids at school. The big barn doors were closed. Head down, and rubbing his cold fingers, Will went inside. His eyes had to adjust after the brightness of the outdoors. The first thing to be done was feed and water Nell, the cart horse.

A scream stopped Will in his tracks. Something massive filled the aisle, a horrible two-headed thing. The boy staggered backward as one of the heads, a thick serpent, raised back to strike at him. At the same time, the other, bigger head screamed another warning. Will was startled by the surprisingly pink diamond of its open mouth.

That was all Will saw. He turned and ran down the narrow lane beside the store. In a nightmare, Will would have frozen, unable to move from the spot, but now he found himself halfway to the road. Then it occurred to him — the men hadn't budged. Worst of all, they were laughing at him.

This made Will angry. He hated to be laughed at. His anger overcame his fear and he marched back into the yard. "What *is* that thing?" he demanded, trying to restore his dignity.

The men continued to laugh while the boy's anger stewed. Whatever the creature was, they obviously weren't afraid of it.

Finally Mr. Sanderson recovered from his mirth, mopping his face with a large handkerchief. "This is Mr. Rufus Peacock, Will," he said. "She belongs to him."

She? Will had never thought of a monster as being female.

Peacock's face fell into its naturally mournful folds. He looked rather like a hound dog, Will thought, but his small eyes were merry. "That, my boy, is an elephant. Toong Talong, by name."

"An elephant?"

Was that how an elephant looked? Will's mouth dropped open. Cap'n Riggs had told them how, in ancient times, Hannibal had used elephants against the Roman army. Will thought back to the monster he had just seen. It would take someone mighty brave to get up on that thing.

"We come up from New York City," said Peacock, "stopping all along the way. Go ahead . . . give 'er another look."

Will opened the door just a crack, ready to slam it if necessary. The thing was truly enormous, bigger even than Chester Honey's prize oxen. It was more like the size of the wagon they pulled, piled high with a load of hay. From what Will could see, it was hairless. He thought it must be cold.

"The only elephant in these United States," Peacock said proudly.

"What are you going to do with it?" Will asked.

Peacock raised his bushy eyebrows as though this would be obvious to anyone. "Scientific education," he said slyly. Will didn't like the way the man winked at him.

"I am presently touring the New England states, putting her on public display. Your employer here . . ." Peacock turned to Mr. Sanderson, "has agreed to allow me the use of his barn."

Will was startled by another trumpeting blast.

Peacock solemnly held his hand over his own stomach. "The call of hunger," he said to explain the elephant's call.

Will looked behind him nervously. "What does she eat?"

Rufus Peacock began to recite. "One hundred and fifty pounds of hay a day, four loaves of bread, several bushels of oats and corn, and all manner of vegetables." Will could tell he had said it many times.

Mr. Sanderson rubbed his hands together. "Will, while you're feeding Nell, pitch down some hay for the elephant."

With all the excitement, Will had forgotten his chores. He looked anxiously down the aisle of the barn where the creature was weaving its head. The serpent part was curled where the nose should be.

"But . . . *it*'s in the way," he said.

Peacock was holding a metal prod that had both a point and a hook on one end. Armed with only this weapon, he walked right into the barn. Will allowed a man had courage to do that. He peeked around the door, curious to see what was going to happen.

With the back of the hook, Peacock pushed against the beast's shoulder. "Toong. Over," he commanded. To Will's amazement, the elephant took a step to the side.

Peacock patted the tough hide. "Gentle as a lamb," he said, mildly.

Still, Will hesitated.

"Come, boy." Peacock's voice was impatient.

One of the elephant's small eyes regarded Will. He tried to determine whether it was a friendly eye. He couldn't be sure. The animal's mouth curled in what looked like a malicious smile. Was it just waiting for him to get within reach? But the nose, if that's what the serpent thing was, only stretched up to the loft and found a wisp of hay.

Will was determined not to be laughed at again. He started down the aisle with the pitchfork clutched in front of him. At least it would be some kind of weapon. Keeping an eye on the elephant's huge feet, he pressed himself close to the wall.

The ears of the beast lifted and flapped like the wings of an angry goose. "PFFUUHH" Her nose swung upward, blowing a fine, slimy spray at him. Will skittered by with a yell. Just as the animal's rope of a tail whipped out, he ducked and scrambled up the ladder to the loft. Keeping out of the elephant's reach, he threw down a pile of hay.

Will stood behind the two men to watch how the elephant scooped up the hay with her nose and pushed it into her mouth. He had never seen anything as strange. There *was* a calf born with two heads over at Buzzard's Cove, but it hadn't lived very long.

The creature seemed to have too much skin. It hung in

sorry folds from her chin and belly and it sagged around the shapeless legs like loose stockings. The animal was gray, except for the tips of the ears and trunk which were pink with spots, and the hide was rough like bark with a sprinkling of coarse, black hairs.

Nell moved restlessly in her stall. Her ears twitched and her eyes were showing their whites. Will made soothing noises, patting the horse's silky neck. As he brought her fresh water, Peacock called for a bucketful for the elephant.

The creature did an astonishing thing with it. She stuck her nose in the bucket and in seconds, the water was gone. Then she squirted it into her mouth.

"It sucked the water up in its nose?" Will asked. "Ugh!"

"Not its nose," Peacock said with dignity. "That is its trunk."

Will frowned at that. The nose thing looked nothing like the boxes in which people stored their clothes.

Then the elephant began shuffling her feet. Squealing, she knocked the empty bucket about. Will backed away, prepared to run. She must be angry about something.

"More water," Peacock ordered. "She has a mighty thirst. We've been traveling all night."

Will hurried to fill the bucket again. It was fascinating, how the water disappeared. Thrilled by this amazing creature, he forgot how tired he was. But after hauling ten more buckets from the pump, his arms felt as though they were pulled out of their sockets, and he could hardly make a fist.

When he finally left the barn, Will was so excited that he almost forgot breakfast. Mrs. Sanderson had some ham and a chunk of cornbread for him to eat on the way to school. The poverty she had seen in Will's home was still vivid in her mind. From then on, she had vowed that Will would not go to school without a good meal.

"Did you see it?" Will asked her.

Lottie shuddered, making the flabby skin under her chin waggle. "Don't want no part of that ungodly thing. Some kinda freak of nature."

"Oh, no," said Will. He crammed some of the cornbread into his mouth. "Mr. Peacock said there are more of them in India." Will wasn't sure where India was; he'd never traveled farther than the next town, but in any case, he knew it was far away from Cadbury.

"Durn them things!" said Mrs. Sanderson, swatting at one of the flies on the counter. "Then India is where it belongs."

Will made no reply, instead he started to leave.

"How's your mother doin'?" Mrs. Sanderson called.

Some of the light left the boy's face as he turned in the doorway. The elephant had driven all thoughts of home from his mind. "She had a bad spell last night. It was hard for her to sleep with the coughing."

Mrs. Sanderson pursed her lips. She didn't like the sound

of it. Her face softened at the boy's earnest expression and she tried to sound encouraging when she told him, "Sometimes those things get better with the cold weather." She took a bottle of tonic from the shelf behind her. "Stop by on the way home and pick up this here syrup. It might do her some good."

Will's mood was less buoyant as he headed off to school. Once again, his mother's racking cough sounded in his head. Still he couldn't wait to tell the others about the elephant. None of them would have seen it yet.

V

Will Volunteers

Will was late for school. In his excitement he blurted out in front of the whole room how he had seen an elephant in Sanderson's barn. The children made fun of his story about the giant beast whose nose hung all the way to the ground, a beast that could make a sound like Gabriel's trumpet.

Cap'n Riggs had not punished Will for telling a lie, but, as a penalty for being tardy, he set him to drawing water from the well during recess and washing the windows.

A small parade followed Will on the way home. Peter Beers was their leader. Holding his nose between thumb and forefinger, Peter sang into Will's ear, "Nah, nah, nah, nah," to the tune of Yankee Doodle.

When Will tried to elbow him away, Peter looked offended. "I'm a elyphunt," he said. "I'm trumpeting!"

The others laughed, thinking this was clever.

"He's tetched, like his mother," Walter Keeler sneered.

His nose was always running, and he wiped it now on the back of his sleeve.

Will thought Walter was one of a group of children who had come by when he and his mother first moved to Tiah's Cove. Even though it was years ago, Will still remembered it. A handful of pebbles had been flung against the door, and when he opened it, the children had run away.

"Tell us again about the elyphunt you saw," urged Peter. *"How* big was it?"

"As big as a house," said Walter Keeler.

"Naw," said Wood Tick. "As big as a barn."

"When are you going to show it to us?" asked Phoebe, Walter's younger sister. Usually, they didn't allow her to walk with them.

Will wouldn't answer. When they got to Sanderson's they'd see, all right.

Peter pointed to a horse cropping grass in Athearn's pasture. "Look," he said to the others. "Maybe that's one of his elyphunts. *Her* nose reaches the ground."

The others laughed again.

An unusual number of wagons stood lined up in front of the general store and a small crowd had gathered outside of the barn.

"Something must've happened," Wood Tick said.

The children forgot about Will and ran to see what it was.

"Hey, look at that," said Walter. Posters with a drawing

of a monstrous animal on them were tacked up on the store.

"It's the elyphunt," said Walter's sister as if she'd known it all along.

Word must have spread quickly. Besides the porch sitters and a lot of children, Will recognized some of the farm families who came in only on Saturday. Mr. Sanderson was standing beside the poster in his white apron, beaming. Crowds like this would be good for business. A tarpaulin hanging across the barn doors hid the elephant from the curious, but from time to time they could hear the swish of hay and a peculiar rumbling.

The children squeezed through the crowd where a rude platform had been thrown up in front of the barn. Above them, Mr. Peacock was speaking in his grand manner. "This wonderful animal will excite the admiration of every beholder," he was saying. "It exceeds anything you have ever seen in size, docility, and sagacity."

Will agreed about the animal's size, but he didn't know what the docility and sagacity part meant. Maybe it had to do with her trunk.

"Ladies and gentlemen!" Mr. Peacock removed his hat, placing it over his heart, and his voice deepened in a way that Will found thrilling. "This creature so far surpasses any description I could ever give you, that I shall not even attempt it at this time. You will have to see it for yourself." With this statement Peacock bowed humbly.

When a few of the curious folks pushed their way to the entrance of the barn, others followed. Leon, the handyman, had been recruited to collect admission.

Snuff and two other dogs that hung around the porch were running through the yard, getting tangled in people's feet. "Here now," Peacock said, waving the animals away. "Don't let those dogs in the barn. It will upset the elephant."

Will shrank back from the pack, but Peter and the other boys were happy to give chase. Walter even picked up a stick and chucked it at the tails of the retreating animals.

Everyone who had paid to see the elephant ducked behind the tarpaulin. The rest waited outside to hear what it was like.

"How much to get in?" Peter asked.

"Twenty-five cents." Leon looked cranky, as usual. "Twelve and a half for children."

Peter turned to Wood Tick. "You got any money?"

"Nah."

"Check your pockets," Peter demanded, seeing the last person disappear behind the tarp.

"I don't got any," the smaller boy squeaked, turning out his pockets.

None of them had the money.

"Let me in," Peter said to Leon. "I'll pay you tomorrow."

Leon shook his head.

"Please? Aw c'mon."

Leon was not moved by Peter's begging. Like Mrs. Sanderson, he didn't believe in giving credit.

Mr. Sanderson had been standing just inside the curtain. "Will," he said pulling it aside, "Come on in. You'll miss the show."

Will was unsure of what to do as he looked first at the storekeeper, and then at the other children.

Sanderson pulled him toward the entrance by the back of the neck.

"Hey, can we come in, too?" asked Peter.

"Friends of yours?" Sanderson asked Will.

Before Will could reply, the storekeeper answered, "Why sure."

Walter was uneasy. "Are we gonna have ta pay for this?" he asked. His father would never give him the money.

Sanderson winked. Word of mouth was good advertising.

"Oh boy!" Walter said, crowding in with Peter. After a second look at the animal on the poster, Wood Tick and Phoebe changed their minds and stayed outside.

The twenty or so who had paid to see hung back as far as they could from the rope that fenced off the elephant. The chains that shackled the huge beast seemed a feeble protection to them. But Will felt a safety in numbers. To show Peter and Walter that he was familiar with elephants, he pushed up to the front.

While Will was in school, Toong Talong had been spruced up. The dust of the road was sponged off and she was wearing a splendid red harness and matching blanket.

Mr. Peacock stood out from the country people in his brocade vest and formal black coat. "Ladies and gentlemen," he began, "I am pleased to present to you the first creature of its kind in these United States. The power of this wonderful animal, which weighs as much as forty fully grown men, cannot be surpassed. It is docile enough to plow a field, or, as it had the occasion to do on this tour, push a loaded coach that was mired down in the mud."

There was a murmur among the farmers, men proud of the strength of their teams. As their interest increased they drifted closer.

Whether out of modesty or boredom, Toong began to shift her weight, restlessly tossing bits of hay over her shoulder. With the first swing of her trunk, the ladies screamed and the crowd parted down the center as the Red Sea had for Moses.

Mr. Peacock went on as if nothing had happened. "The elephant is among the most intelligent of animals," he said. "Like the domestic cat and dog, it has developed an affection for man. Nevertheless . . ." Peacock raised a cautionary finger, "if aroused to anger by brutal treatment, it would split the human skull with a single flick of its trunk."

As these words, there was a gasp from the crowd, and more than one mother pulled back her curious youngsters. Will moaned, remembering how close he had come to that skull-splitting trunk.

To reassure the audience, Peacock slipped under the

rope and began to stroke Toong's trunk. "With this unique appendage," he said, "the elephant has been known to untie a knot, lift a four-hundred-pound load, or . . ." Peacock removed a few grains of popcorn from his pocket and dropped them on the floor. Toong immediately snatched them up and deposited them in her mouth.

". . . or clean your rug."

Some in the audience tittered nervously.

"Now . . ." Peacock stroked his gilded vest. "May I ask for someone in the audience to assist me?"

There was silence. The folks in front turned around to check the people behind them. Peter scuffled good-naturedly with Walter Keeler, as each tried to shove the other forward. Everyone looked at someone else, but no one was willing to volunteer.

"Ladies and gentlemen," Peacock assured them. "This animal has traveled by ship from its home in India. From London to New York and across the length and breadth of New England, it has never hurt a living soul."

There were whispers of amazement.

While scanning the audience, Mr. Peacock recognized Will. "You, young man. Come up here."

Except for the elephant, who was blowing through her trunk, the barn grew silent again.

Will hoped the man meant someone else. He looked around at Peter and Walter who went pale.

"You, right here in front," Peacock said, pointing to him.

"Me?" Will asked weakly.

"Come up."

All eyes were now on the boy. Mr. Sanderson caught his eye and nodded.

Will stepped forward and ducked under the rope. Putting his arm around the boy's shoulders, Peacock drew him toward the elephant. This seemed to make the creature more agitated and she let out one of her trumpeting bellows. At this, Will pulled back but the man had a firm grip on his arm.

The boy's bowels weakened at the sight of the elephant towering over him and he felt an overwhelming urge to visit the privy. He had forgotten how terrifying it was to come within reach of that trunk. Two faces mocked him from the second row. Walter and Peter were laughing. By Monday, the whole school would know how frightened he was and he would never hear the end of it.

"Young man," Peacock said. "This elephant, who is reputed to be among the wisest of the animals, tells me you have brought it a present. One of its favorites, in fact."

Will was shocked. "N-no," he stammered, shaking his head. "I didn't bring nothin'." He held out his empty hands. "Not me."

Mr. Peacock turned to the elephant. Its trunk was sampling the air between them and its head nodded up and down as if to say yes.

"Do you mind if she checks?" Peacock looked around at the audience and grinned. Everyone waited for Will's answer. Now that he was the victim, they were enjoying the scene.

Will gave Mr. Sanderson a desperate look. Peacock had moved aside, leaving him alone in front of the beast. She took a step forward and began to run her snuffling trunk over his jacket. Will shut his eyes, afraid to make the slightest movement of any kind, even to breathe, lest it upset her. When she came to his jacket pocket she dipped her trunk in and withdrew something.

"Hey." Walter craned his neck to see. "It's gingerbread," he shouted.

Will could smell it. His eyes flew open. It *was* gingerbread, the kind Mrs. Sanderson kept on the counter.

"I never took any," he said.

The elephant popped the gingerbread into her mouth. Everyone laughed except Will who stared in amazement. How did the gingerbread get into his pocket?

Mr. Peacock stepped forward again. "Gingerbread gives me a thirst," he said. "What about you folks?" And he placed a bottle of ale on the elephant's broad head.

Gurgling with pleasure, the animal reached up for it. She removed the cork with the greatest delicacy and drank the contents of the bottle.

The audience laughed.

"Godfrey," Peter said in astonishment.

Will was so fascinated he forgot to escape while he had the chance.

Then Peacock picked up the prod. "Now Toong, what

do we say to these nice people?" He turned his back to the audience, and only Will heard him speak to the elephant. "Toong. Down. Down." At the same time he was pushing against her front legs with the prod.

The elephant's legs were as thick and shapeless as beech trunks. Very slowly, one knee bent and then the other, and she sank down in a reluctant bow.

The audience began to clap.

Will's own legs trembled with relief. But when he looked at the other boys, he swelled with a feeling of importance. For the first time in his life he saw envy in their eyes.

*

Will's face was still flushed with excitement when he got home, but at the sight of his mother, he stopped short. He had forgotten to get the syrup from Mrs. Sanderson. But Maddy seemed more like herself today, and she was charmed with Will's story about Mr. Peacock and the elephant.

"He told everyone that I brought it a present, you see. And when no one was lookin', he must've stuck this piece of gingerbread in my pocket."

Maddy clasped her hands together. "Will, how wonderful."

Then she tilted her head to one side, listening. "Shh."

They went to the open door where the sun was slanting in. All Will heard was the sound of crickets.

"What is it?" he asked.

"Just listen."

From far off, came a squawking sound that grew closer. Will could see the V formation against the pale sky, each bird calling its position.

"They're only geese," he said. "They come every fall." What was so wonderful about them? he wondered. They weren't special like the elephant.

The voices swelled louder as the geese passed over them.

Maddy leaned her head against the door jamb until the sound faded. Will was stricken to see that her eyes were bright with tears.

"Mother! What is it?" he asked.

"Nothing." Maddy caressed his upturned cheek. "It's just the fever," she said. "It leaves me weepy."

VI

Beauty and the Beast

The following morning Will stood in front of the store giving out handbills advertising the elephant. Saturday at Sanderson's was always busy. While the farm wives traded their surplus eggs and butter for dry goods, their husbands dealt with Sanderson in the back room. Few farmers had cash, and so their debts were paid off with potatoes, corn, and oats.

By closing time, Will thought everyone in Cadbury must have seen the elephant. A heavy fog was rolling in from the sound but a few curious folks still lingered. One large family had even bartered a jug of homemade rum for the price of admission. Peacock's ringing voice was drawing the last of them into the barn when Maddy appeared out of the mist, wearing her flowered shawl.

Will was surprised and happy to see her looking so well; she had been so listless since she was ill. Now her eyes sparkled with excitement like a young girl's. "I picked these for the elephant," she said breathlessly, setting down a basket of wild grapes.

Will took the heavy basket and led Maddy around to the lower level of the barn where Peacock was getting ready for the last performance. "Sir," he said, holding out the basket of grapes, "My mother brought these for the elephant."

"Splendid. Splendid."

Peacock went on scrubbing at the splashes of manure that had dried on his trousers. But when he saw how pretty the young woman was, her red hair haloed in lantern light, he straightened up with interest.

Rubbing his lower lip, he considered her. At last he said in an oily voice, "I would be pleased to have you at the lecture if you would be my guest."

Maddy clasped her hands in delight.

Peacock guided her up the ladder and Will followed them to where a hushed crowd was waiting. In the flickering light, Toong Talong loomed even more monstrous than before.

Will stood in the shadows with his mother. "Oh!" she breathed, clutching Will's hand. "Oh, how wonderful!" Maddy was struck by awe of the elephant, but she didn't seem afraid.

Peacock delivered his usual speech, which was now familiar to Will. But this time he didn't ask for a volunteer.

"I see you have brought the elephant a present," he said to Maddy, and he beckoned her to come forward.

As his mother stepped into the light, Will remembered the last time she had shown herself in the village. Just as he feared, heads nodded together and a stir went through the audience when they recognized her. Will shrank deeper into the shadows.

Maddy hesitated until Peacock gestured for her to give the grapes to the elephant.

No one dared breathe. Even Will forgot his embarrassment as his mother went closer. He chewed his lip with suspense.

The elephant bobbed its head. Everyone marveled at how Maddy fearlessly held the basket, never flinching as Toong Talong reached for some grapes and put them into her mouth. Bunch after bunch, the elephant took the grapes until they were gone.

Then Peacock swept his arms with a flourish, "Beauty and the Beast, ladies and gentlemen."

Will turned toward the audience when they applauded, swelling with pride in his mother.

Toong swept her trunk over the floor, picking up spilled grapes. Then she curled it up and squealed. Her mouth was open for more.

Maddy reached out and tickled the pale pink tongue.

"Uh!" Two boys up front made faces.

Maddy was delighted as the elephant stretched forward

for more scratching. "She likes it," she said.

Horrified, a woman turned away with her hand at her throat. "How could you!"

"Her tongue feels nice . . . like a pillow," Maddy said. Her face lit up when she thought of a comparison. "Like Mrs. Snokes's silk dress."

The farmers guffawed and even their wives had to smother giggles. Plump Mrs. Snokes was the minister's wife.

Peacock tried to get back their attention. "Grapes give me a thirst," he said, loudly. "How about you folks?" But they were still laughing over what Maddy had said.

Will wanted to shout at them, "Shut up you stupid people!" Didn't they understand — his mother had done something brave and now they were laughing at her.

*

When Will came to work on Monday he emptied the mousetraps and hurried as he swept out the store. Peacock would be leaving today and this would be Will's last chance to see the elephant. The cat was curled up asleep in the sack of oatmeal. Will shooed it out as Mrs. Sanderson came downstairs with a plate of hot mush and apple pie.

"If that don't beat all," she muttered, slamming down Will's plate. "Harborin' a thing like that is just beggin' for trouble."

Will didn't ask what was wrong. In Mrs. Sanderson's view, most everything was.

Her husband came in from the barn and checked the vegetable bins. "We need more onions," he said. "She's got a chill."

Will looked up from his slab of pie. "The elephant is sick?"

"Oh land o' mercy." Mrs. Sanderson raised her eyes toward Heaven. "It's gonna eat us out of house and home."

But Sanderson was cheerful. "It all goes on the account, my dear. Peacock already gave me an advance toward her keep."

Mrs. Sanderson snorted. Her husband was known to be a shrewd dealer but sometimes his sociability got in the way of his sense.

The storekeeper looked at Will over the tops of his glasses. "Bring up one of those baskets of onions, will you?" And he went out back again.

"I tell ya . . ." his wife called after him, ". . . a creature like that don't belong here." She stared after Sanderson, shaking her head. "That Peacock feller is just dumpin' it on us."

Will couldn't believe what he'd just heard. "You're going to keep the elephant here?" he asked.

Lottie gave his plate an angry shove. "Peacock can't walk it round no more till spring," she said. "That jungle thing ain't made for the cold."

Will hustled down to the cellar. He was often sent there

to replenish Sanderson's stock and it was one of his favorite places. He loved the way the mellow scent of apples mixed with the smell of smoked fish and pickles. Dark, smoky hams hung from the low ceilings. Overhead, the floorboards squeaked under the tread of customers and he could hear their muffled voices.

Being alone with all this plenty felt good to Will, like a miser surrounded by gold, but today he didn't linger. Full of excitement, he struggled upstairs with a basket of onions and lugged it out to the barn.

There stood the elephant, drooping and runny-eyed, wrapped in a patchwork of blankets. She had only scattered the hay Leon had pitched down for her that morning. Mrs. Sanderson was right. Traveling during the cold nights of a New England autumn had made the animal sick. Sanderson and Peacock were discussing her care while Leon leaned on his pitchfork.

Will set down the basket.

"Ah! These'll do the trick," said Peacock, rubbing his hands together. "A sure cure. Sure cure. Onions warm her right up. You'll see."

The elephant snuffled about the basket. She popped one of the onions in her mouth, then another with great relish, as though she were polishing off a bowl of cherries. Will watched with fascination as the entire basketful disappeared.

Peacock asked Leon to saddle his horse. Then he walked

the elephant out of the barn and down to a large stall on the lower floor where a few cows were kept. That part of the barn had been built into the hillside and caught the slanting rays of the winter sun. Even the water buckets never froze there.

"Where are you headed for now?" Sanderson asked Peacock as the boy and the two men stood watching the elephant.

"Well . . ." Peacock stretched his chin and gazed at the ceiling, like a man contemplating adventure. "Thought I might look up a fellow I ran into in Providence." He rocked back on his heels. "He had a few opportunities for a man who wished to make an investment."

Will licked his lips. Providence sounded as good as India to him. He followed the men as they strolled out to the yard. Hoots and hollers came from the road as children passed by the store. It was time for school already. Will clenched his fists with impatience. He wanted to hear the rest of the men's conversation.

Just then, Leon led a horse around from the upper part of the barn, a chestnut with a white blaze.

"Godfrey!" Will said in admiration. "Is he yours?"

Peacock smiled with satisfaction. "Made the transaction just yesterday."

The school bell was ringing. Will backed away, his eyes on the splendid horse.

Peacock shook hands with Sanderson. "See you in the spring," he said, swinging into the saddle. "Remember, there's nothing to keeping an elephant. Just so long as she knows who's boss."

If Peacock meant the beast they had just been watching in the barn, Will doubted it would be so easy.

*

The onion cure worked, but Will's doubts were correct; it was no simple task to care for the elephant. That was Leon's job, but for some reason, the elephant took a dislike to him. Toong could hold an entire bucketful of water in her trunk, and even after she had put it in her mouth and swallowed, she would bring some of it back up again to spray at the handyman. Leon swore at the elephant, calling her a devil, but Will thought he saw a spark of humor under her long lashes.

One day Toong hit Leon with the side of her head. Luckily, he was standing close and the blow only knocked him to the ground. If the elephant had gotten a wider swing she might have broken bones.

The next morning Leon quit. Will heard the Sandersons discussing it while he was cleaning the ashes from the stove.

"I warned you," Mrs. Sanderson said to her husband. "Some night that thing'll bring the house down around our heads."

But Mrs. Sanderson was happy to see Leon go. In her opinion, he was the worst of the no-good loafers Sanderson put up with.

The storekeeper reasoned with her. "Leon don't cost much to keep," he said, "just room and board. Besides, where would he go?"

Leon had come with the store when they bought it thirty years ago, and he'd seemed old even then. "The man has his pride," Sanderson said. "I'll ask him to stay."

The storekeeper saw Will listening. "The boy here is young and strong," he said. "Maybe he'd come back after school and give Leon a hand."

Will nodded eagerly. He could use the extra wages.

From then on he spent more time in the barn with the elephant. Every day she turned a small mountain of food into a flood of foul-smelling manure that Will had to clean up. It made him even less popular at school. Any boy unlucky enough to sit next to him would lean away, holding his nose and rolling his eyes until the others snickered. Will told himself he didn't care, so long as the boys left him alone.

*

One afternoon Peter and his friends stopped to look at the elephant after school. They hung back in the doorway, watching as Will watered her, and each time she raised her dripping trunk they yelled and backed away. Will began to enjoy having an audience, especially since he was in command here. He even let Wood Tick carry one of the buckets for him.

"Look out," Will warned importantly when the boy got

too close. "Don't come up behind her like that. It makes her nervous when she don't see you."

In a few days Peter and the others came again. Will gave them bunches of hay to toss to the elephant. Soon the three boys stopped almost every day. Although they still weren't friendly with Will at school, they no longer bothered him there.

When they became bored watching Toong eat hay, the boys saved treats from their lunches. At first they tossed her the bits of bread and apples. Then they grew bold, daring each other to let her take it out of their hands.

Peter discovered that the elephant was fond of eating tobacco. The next time he came he had snitched one of his father's cigars for her.

Just as Peter was about to feed Toong the cigar, he had an idea. "Watch this," he said, "I'll light it for her." And he lit the cigar, puffing on it to get it started.

Walter Keeler giggled nervously, stepping back from the elephant's reaching trunk. Will was outside filling the water buckets.

Wood Tick was frightened. "You better not. You'll get us in trouble," he hissed.

At that moment Will came into the barn. "Hey! What're you doin'?" His buckets clunked to the ground, splashing water.

"Nothin'," Peter said innocently. "We was just sneakin' a smoke."

Full of outrage at what Peter was doing, Will snatched the cigar and threw it down, grinding it out with his bare heel.

"Get out," Will shouted, angrily. "And don't come around here no more."

"What's the fuss?" Peter shrugged as he was leaving. "We didn't hurt nothin'."

A painful throb started in Will's heel. In his fury he hadn't even felt the heat when he ground out the cigar, but now he was trembling. Peter was much bigger than he was. What if he had refused to go?

VII

Losing Maddy

At first Will was fooled into thinking his mother was getting better because she grew more beautiful. Maddy's eyes were bright and her skin was flushed with fever. Her cheeks and her cloud of coppery hair were the only vivid colors in their downstairs room.

Indian summer came and her cough worsened. The days were warmer, but Maddy went out less, even though she loved the woods. Alarmed that she was so thin, Will set snares in the woods to catch animals. He tried to tempt her with a plump rabbit but she had no interest in food.

When the trees lost their leaves, a change came over Maddy. She was excited by their skeleton shadows on the wall. The grapevines still lay untouched in the corner, but now she wanted to draw. To make his mother happy, Will brought her wrapping paper from the store. He had the good luck to snare a wild turkey and he cut pen points for her from its quills.

Maddy steeped ink from the bark of swamp maples. While Will was gone all day, she worked feverishly, filling the brown sheets he had brought her with twisted oak forms, weaving deer, quail, and crouching rabbits among their branches. By the end of the week, the house was littered with drawings. When Will opened the door they scattered like dead leaves across the floor.

After that burst of energy, Maddy was exhausted. Her sleep was fitful, with alternating sweats and chills. Bone tired, Will did all the chores, thinking if he was good and worked hard, she would get well. He tried not to wake her when he left in the morning and each night he returned hoping that she would be better.

One clear November night, Will woke with a start. He saw that it must be late, the moon was well across the sky. Maddy's breathing was so hoarse that he could hear it on his side of the loft. Will lit a piece of candle and stood shivering next to her bed. "Is it bad tonight?" he whispered, leaning over her.

Maddy coughed. Her hand flew to her lips and to Will's horror, bright blood spilled between her fingers.

"Mother!" he cried out.

"Don't leave me," she pleaded, clutching his sleeve, but he pulled away.

"I have to get help," he told her. When he backed down the ladder, she was still coughing.

The stars shook as he ran, all the way to the Sandersons'. "I'm sorry. I'm sorry." He said it over and over, gasping as his mother had, feet slapping loud on the empty road. "I'm sorry, Mother." He shouldn't have left her, he thought, but the blood was so frightening.

Will rounded Brandy Brow. He saw no lights anywhere. The windows were dark over the store, but he pounded on the door till Mr. Sanderson came down.

The storekeeper listened to his story, jamming the tails of his nightshirt into his trousers. The pale figure of Mrs. Sanderson hovered at the top of the stairs.

"What's goin' on?" she called down.

"It's Will," Sanderson said. "His mother's been taken worse. I'm goin' to Barnstable for the doctor."

Would the doctor come to his house? Hearing this excited Will, but at the same time it troubled him. He had seen the doctor's carriage in front of houses before someone died.

Sanderson gave Will a gentle shove toward the stairs. "You go on up," he said.

Will had never been upstairs over the store. He sat in the Sandersons' kitchen while Mrs. Sanderson dressed. She was going back with him.

Now that his sweat had dried, Will shook like a pup on the edge of the rocker. He thought about his mother being alone, and he grew more anxious as he waited, nervously rubbing at the legs of his trousers until his palms tingled.

At last Mrs. Sanderson was ready. Will could see the

little puffs of her breath as she labored down the road. It was agony to slow down to her pace but he was glad she was coming home with him. He was afraid to be alone with his mother when she was like that.

The little house seemed ominously dark and still, so still that the click of the door latch was jarring to Will.

He looked fearfully at the loft, relieved to see the candle he had left was still burning. His eyes pleaded with Mrs. Sanderson to go up first, but as she toiled up the ladder he stayed downstairs, poking life back into the fire.

Mrs. Sanderson was talking up there. Will strained to hear his mother. He relaxed some at the sound of her voice.

Not long after that he heard the doctor's carriage outside and he ran to open the door for him. Will started to speak but the doctor pushed past with only a nod. He was an older man and heavyset. A gold watch chain swung from his belly as he climbed to the loft and the rungs creaked under his weight.

Will was still standing watch at the foot of the ladder when Mr. Sanderson arrived. The storekeeper looked old tonight, his cheeks sunken, maybe because his usually jovial expression was missing. He and Will waited together in front of the fire. Mr. Sanderson was strangely silent. Now and then the man sighed and cleared his throat noisily. Once he got up and looked out the window. Before he sat down again, he squeezed Will's shoulder. Will would have felt easier if the storekeeper had talked some and joked with him the way he did with the men in the back room of the store; the situation would not seem so grave.

Mrs. Sanderson called to her husband and there was a small disturbance as the men dismantled Maddy's bed and moved it downstairs. It was hard for Will to believe that the still form they lowered in a blanket was his mother; how had she become so small?

By then it was daybreak. The doctor left and Mr. Sanderson had to open the store. "Don't bother about work, today," he said to Will. Otherwise, none of them paid him much attention.

The doctor had left Mrs. Sanderson some powders to mix with water. She fussed at the bedside, sponging Maddy's face and making little coaxing noises as she urged her to take sips of the doctor's brew. But the hours passed slowly for Will. He sat at the window, avoiding the sight of his mother's bed, and tried not to fidget. No one had told him what was going to happen. Would his mother be all right? He was afraid to break the silence by asking. Some delicate balance might be upset and start his mother coughing. Will's whole life seemed to be coming to an end, yet outside the sun went on shining.

Toward noon, Reverend Snokes came. He brought along Mrs. Snokes whose watery eyes and soft, downy face were gently disapproving. She put Butternut and the chickens out. They couldn't have animals in the room, she said.

Maddy's bed and her sickness and the women filled the house until there didn't seem to be any place for Will. He went outside to find flowers for his mother, but the dusty asters along the road had faded. Then he huddled in the sunny doorway with a small bunch of bittersweet in his hand. He sat there, sheltered from the wind until Mrs. Snokes called him in to see his mother.

Will was shocked by how different Maddy looked. Her wiry hair had been tamed into braids and the women had dressed her in someone's clean gown. Her hands on the sheet were colorless like the unbleached muslin.

Will knelt and touched her fingers. "Mother?" he said, timidly.

She didn't seem to see him, but the fingers under his hand fluttered. Suddenly the fluttering stopped.

Mrs. Snokes leaned close to his mother. Then her pale eyes rose to meet Will's. He took a deep breath to ask the question, "Is she gone?" but barely a sound came out of him, just a whimper.

Mrs. Snokes nodded.

Will buried his face as the minister said a prayer over Maddy.

"Will." Mrs. Sanderson laid a hand on his shoulder. "Reverend Snokes has offered to take you to our house."

Feeling numb, Will rose to his feet. He didn't know why he had to leave except they told him it was so.

"The Reverend is waiting," his wife announced. Her

back was very straight and her white hands were folded across her waist. "Would you like me to help pack your things?"

"No, Ma'am," Will croaked, keeping his back to her. What was there to bring? He stood up and walked blindly toward the door, his eyes brimming with tears. If he took a last look at his mother, he knew they would spill over.

*

That night Will lay in the Sandersons' kitchen, listening to the unfamiliar tick of a clock. He had never slept anywhere but home before.

Now and then, with suddenness, cinders dropped in the grate. A wagon rattled by, the sound fading down South Road. Will couldn't believe that his mother was gone. He thought about her lying in the empty house. Did she know he wasn't there now?

The idea struck him with such urgency that he sat up. Maybe his mother wasn't really dead. Suppose the women were mistaken? He had even heard of people being buried alive. She could be lying there in the dark, helpless and afraid. The ashes in the fireplace would be cold now and she wouldn't know where he'd gone.

Will slipped out of bed, his heart pounding with hope. He must be quiet. Forcing himself to move slowly, he slipped his clothes from the chair. If the Sandersons woke they would stop him, and he had to see his mother.

He dressed in a hurry, impatient with the buttons. Trying not to make a sound, he tiptoed across the kitchen and down the stairs. Outside, the moon was full, whitewashing the orchard. He could easily be seen. Will kept to the shadows until the general store was out of sight. Then he ran the rest of the way home.

The little house stood alone in its clearing, silvery under the moon. Now that he was here, Will felt frightened. Timid, he pressed the latch. As the door swung in, a patch of moonlight spread across the floorboards to Maddy's bed.

She was there. Tears flooded Will's eyes. He hadn't known how powerfully the sight of her would strike him. When the door was shut the two of them were in shadow again.

Will stood beside his mother. Her eyes were closed and her hands crossed peacefully on her breast.

"Mother," he said, gently, the way he'd wake her when he had a nightmare. "Mother?" He didn't want to startle her but he needed comforting.

Gently, Will touched her face, just brushing her cheek with the backs of his fingers. Her skin was so cold that his hand pulled away. Grief rose in Will's throat. The lump was so hard that he could not swallow.

"Oh Mother, no." He sank beside her and wept.

When Will was calm, he brought a chair over and sat with her. The moonlight crept across the wall and over her pillow, putting him in a kind of weary trance.

Later, there was a loud thump against the window.

Will started.

Someone was looking in . . . a devil's head with horns and pointed ears. "Butternut."

Will ran to let her in. The goat's rope had been chewed through. Her tail wagged happily as she followed him out to the chicken coop. Inside the shelter, Will made out the sleeping forms on their roost. At first the hens flapped and squawked as he lifted them, but he stroked down their feathers, soothing them with his voice. Two at a time, he carried them into the house, one under each arm.

Before the gray dawn settled into all the corners of the room, Will had undone his mother's hair and spread it like the sun around her head. He hadn't had a chance to give her the bittersweet. Now he took the bunch from the cracked cup on the table and laid it on her breast. That was how she was when Mr. Sanderson came looking for him, with the doors open to the sun and the hens fluttering across the sill.

The storekeeper took Will by the hand and sat down with him on the doorstep. "Do you have anyone to stay with?" he asked the boy.

"I'm stayin' here," Will said, stubbornly.

"No, Will," Sanderson's voice was patient. "This house belongs to the bank. And they're going to want it back."

Will looked up at the curled and weatherstained shingles. He'd always thought it was their house, his and his mother's.

"Do you have any family? Some folks of your mother's to go to?"

Will shook his head no.

"Did your mother tell you where your pa is?" the store-keeper asked.

Will shook his head in misery.

"Well then, you'll stay with us."

It was odd, Will thought as he rode away with Mr. Sanderson. Sanderson's store was the place he had always wanted to be before. But that was when he had a home to go back to.

That afternoon before the burial, Mr. Sanderson told Will to choose some boots from the store bin. They were the first new pair he had ever owned. Sanderson said they would fit better when they got used to him.

The Sandersons walked with him from the store to the cemetery. Will didn't know what to expect. He was surprised that a little group of people were waiting there with Reverend Snopes.

Will almost panicked when he saw the open grave — the coffin would be down there. But Mrs. Sanderson put her arm around his shoulder and led him forward.

Will bowed his head with the others, but he kept his eyes on the new boots he was wearing, careful not to listen to the minister's words about God or his mother. He didn't want to look down in that hole or think of her being there. That way, he wouldn't feel anything.

Will jumped in surprise. The Reverend Snopes had dropped a handful of earth on the coffin. Will looked down at the wooden box. They were going to cover Maddy with dirt, he thought, and he would never, never see her again.

*

Will stood in the doorway of Leon's room in the barn. What light there was came from a small window near the ceiling. It had been a tackroom once, and it was spare and narrow like the old handyman. From now on, Will would have to sleep there, in a strange bed.

"That one's yours." Leon gave a nod toward the upper bunk.

Will took off his jacket and hung it on a nail next to the door. Then he pulled off the new boots and placed them side by side on the floor. Without a word, he climbed into the bunk and curled up with his face to the wall.

VIII

The Elephant in the Dark

"**W**ill, help me!"

His mother was floating in the brook next to the house, her bright hair spreading around her. Will tried to follow as the brook carried her away, but brambles and the outcropping rocks kept him back from the shore. His movements were slow and heavy. Then he came upon a deep pool where his name echoed, spreading out like ripples over the water. There he saw the pale moon of her face gleaming beneath the surface. He stretched out his hand but she was sinking deeper, deeper until she was gone from him.

Flinging out his arm, Will felt rough boards next to his face. He sat up, bumping his head. Then he knew where he was, Leon's room, where he slept. Now he was awake, but the dream still surrounded him in the darkness. Will looked toward the window to fend off the frightening images. I never should have left her, he thought . . . that night when she needed me. He kept his eyes fixed on the pale square of light until the nightmare faded.

Will lay back. Below him, Leon snored. Had Grandfather snored like that? He couldn't remember, he was so little then. They were both gone now, Grandfather and Mother. He felt under the mattress to make sure her drawings were there. Except for them, there was nothing left of hers. Even Butternut and the chickens had been sold. Hot tears welled up and trickled their way into Will's ears. He was so lonely without Maddy he wished that he were dead, too.

The snoring sputtered and stopped. Leon cleared his throat. Will scrubbed at his eyes with his sleeve and waited for the old man to cough and then lean over, as he did every morning, to hawk and spit into the chamber pot. When Leon's knotted white legs swung over the side of the bunk, it would be time to get up.

None of that happened. Will leaned toward the window. The stars were bright; it must still be early. He shivered. It was cold in here. Will reached for his trousers at the foot of his bed and put them on. Climbing down from the bunk, he gathered up his shoes and his blanket and slipped out.

Hearing him, Nell rattled her feed bucket, thinking it was time for breakfast. Will could barely see the mare's dark head as she lifted it over her stall door. He scratched her between the eyes and laid his cheek on her soft nose.

Then he felt his way to the ladder and climbed down to the lower floor.

It was warm down there and the smell of hay and the softly breathing animals comforted him. Toong shifted her feet. Will made out the hump of her back and the high, lumpy forehead. The next stall was empty. He curled up on a pile of hay, and covered himself. Just before Will drifted into sleep he heard the elephant blow through her trunk. It was a sigh, maybe.

The lowing of the cows woke Will and he rolled over. Slowly, his eyes opened. Then he froze. The elephant was towering over him. Will scuttled sideways like a crab, tangling himself in the blanket. How had she gotten in here?

"Git. Git back there," Will yelled.

Deep in her throat, the elephant rumbled.

"Git back in yer stall!" Will commanded again. His heart was thumping.

The elephant backed up a step.

Will scrambled out the door and slammed it shut. He was sure he had bolted her door last night. Lucky he had found out about it in time. Leon would be furious.

*

Toong was getting restless, penned up as she was. Anything left in her stall, such as a water bucket, she stomped on or crushed between her enormous molars. Later that week she broke a shovel and Will spent an evening watching Leon put on a new handle.

A few days after that he heard banging inside the barn.

"Aaagh! That's where it is," Leon was yelling over the din. "Stop that, you devil."

The pounding went on. Will hurried inside to the elephant's stall. "What's happening?"

Leon turned his rage on the boy. "I've been lookin' fer that shovel all day. You went and forgot it again."

Now Toong was pounding the wall with it. Will's heart sank. He'd been careless.

The shovel clanged to the ground and the elephant reached out toward Will. "I'll get it," he said hastily. Before she picked up the shovel again, Will grabbed the prod and opened the door.

"Watch out," Leon warned. Since the time the elephant had knocked him down, he refused to get in the stall with her.

Will pushed the door closed behind him, keeping his eyes on the elephant. The shovel lay where she had dropped it, between her feet. "Nice girl," he said. "You don't really want that shovel, do you."

Will hoped Toong couldn't hear the fear in his voice. He wished he could tell what she was thinking. He didn't want to believe that she would hurt him, but one kick or swipe with her trunk could be lethal. Even her tail was dangerous.

The elephant watched him out of the corner of her eye.

Will took a deep breath. "Over," he said, pushing the prod against her shoulder.

She didn't move.

The elephant had to know who was boss, Peacock had said. Will commanded more firmly, "Toong, over." And he pushed harder this time.

There was a slap and splash of dung falling. The elephant shifted her weight. Then, reluctantly, she moved over.

Keeping the prod raised as if he could ward off a blow, Will ducked down and grabbed the shovel with his other hand. "Good. Good, girl," he said, backing away. He had almost made it. Feeling behind him, he opened the door and slipped out.

"Here," Will said, passing the shovel to Leon. His legs went so weak he had to lean on the door. At the same time he was elated. He felt a power he'd never owned before. The elephant had obeyed him.

*

The first snow fell in December, big wet flakes that piled up quickly. Sudden gusts whipped the snow into a frenzied dance and set the trees bobbing. The barn walls creaked as the wind leaned against them like a heavy animal.

Next morning the village was muffled in a blanket of white. The sky was a clear blue and the sun on the snow was blinding as Will and Leon dug out. The boy stopped for a moment to look toward the distant trees glittering with ice. Today, more than ever, he longed for home. Sunshine would be flooding the little house in the woods and hungry birds would be waiting at the sill to be fed. At least, Will thought with some satisfaction, no one else was living there. It was still his house, he felt—his and his mother's.

Midmorning Will heard harness bells. Soon the stable yard was lined with ox teams, blowing and stamping. The roads had been broken out.

Sanderson sent him down to the cellar for cider. Loud boots stamped on the floor above, and the store rocked with male laughter. Hearing their hearty voices, Will felt even more alone.

The gray days of January followed, one after the other. The manure pile steamed and the mud froze. Except in the most bitter weather, the horse and cows in their thick winter coats stayed outside, but the elephant had to be kept in the barn. It was a good thing she was willing, because Leon and Will couldn't make her do anything unless she wanted to.

Toong's hide was beginning to crack like old leather. Will could hear her scratching the rough brown patches against the stall. He thought it might help if he rubbed her down with neat's-foot oil. Leon used it to keep harness soft. Toong enjoyed his attentions, swaying slightly, eyes

shut, while he worked in the oil with a rag.

Will had moved his mattress down to the vacant stall. Sleep came easier with the sounds of the animals around him, and sleep was a way to forget his loneliness—except when he dreamed again of losing his mother. Then the feeling of despair would be waiting the next night as soon as his head touched the pillow.

Toong had learned to unfasten her door. Having the boy nearby seemed to soothe the elephant. Blowing softly, she would run the tip of her trunk over Will's blanket and hair. Now, every night when he woke from a bad dream, she was standing over him like a guardian angel. Sometimes she was dozing.

Will saw that the elephant was getting lame. It was her toenails that gave her pain. Shut up as she was, they hadn't worn down the way they would if she was living in the wild.

Will took Leon's wood rasp from the workbench. Remembering the trick she had performed with Peacock, he nudged her leg with the prod. "Toong. Foot," he commanded. Patiently, he persisted until she picked up her foot.

He tried, gingerly at first, to file down one of her nails. Toong didn't seem to mind, as though she knew he was helping her. She learned to hold her foot steady while he worked on one every day. It was a hard job; her nails were as solid as bone. But Will was touched by how such a powerful creature depended on him.

He had not gone back to school after his mother died. Many of the bigger boys and girls stayed home when they were needed. Secretly Will was glad that the Sandersons needed him. Now he only had to see Peter and the other boys when they came in the store, and they didn't bother him there.

Every day the elephant consumed over two hundred pounds of food. Will pitched down their winter's supply of hay until it was all gone. Then Sanderson had to buy more at a high price.

"I warned you," Lottie scolded when Peacock failed to send the promised money.

"Don't worry," the storekeeper said. "We'll hear from him soon. Besides, the elephant's good for business. Such a curiosity brings in customers."

It was true that strangers had heard of the elephant and they stopped at Sanderson's instead of passing straight through town. On shopping days, farm families craned their necks in the barn doorway, hoping for a glimpse of Toong. So did the children on the way home from school, and it made Will feel important.

He knew that Sanderson was worried. Will saw how the storekeeper would check the levels of hay and grain and go off shaking his head, but Sanderson remained cheerful in front of Lottie. "Spring will be here before you know it," he said, "and then the elephant will be gone."

Already, the ground was thawing; across the road, Athearn's wagon stood axle-deep in mud. Will realized now how badly he was going to miss the elephant. There wasn't much time left before Peacock would come and take her away.

IX

Toong Breaks Loose

By the first of March, the daffodils were three inches high in the sheltered dooryard behind the store. There was a surprise snowfall that night but the next day was mild and sunny. Will felt so warm he took off his jacket. From the maple, hundreds of blackbirds chirped in rusty chorus. They all flew off at the clank of the pump handle and the tree seemed to rise with them, free of its burden. For the first time since his mother died, Will's heart sang.

He set the water down while he opened the barn door. The boy had grown taller over the winter and filled out some. Now he could carry two heavy buckets at once.

Splat! Something hit the inside of the window.

"Whoa there. Now stop that," Will called out, but he had to smile. Toong had made a discovery — manure hit the window with the satisfying sound of a wet snowball.

Cautiously Will opened the door. "Think that's funny, don't you."

While Toong drank, he scrubbed at the dirty window with a handful of straw. Outside, the eaves were dripping, and with a sudden swoosh, melting snow slid from the roof and hit the ground.

Leon pushed open the door, stamping off snow on the hard-packed dirt floor.

"Think we could let her out for a while?" Will asked him. "It's so warm. Any minute now, she's gonna bust out."

Leon looked uncertain.

"Hey!" he suddenly yelled.

With a deft swipe, Toong had snatched the greasy cap the old man wore winter and summer. Will rescued it on the way to her mouth.

Leon muttered an oath. "All right. Go ahead." He gave the boy a grim nod. With the cap pulled down, Leon's ears stood out even more than usual.

Throwing open the doors, Will led the elephant out into blinding sunlight.

Toong set her feet down gingerly in the snow. Uncertain, she tested it with her trunk. With a squeak of surprise, she blew out the cold, wet stuff. She tried eating some, as she did with a lot of new things. Then she kicked the snow and swung at it with her trunk, whipping showers into the air until the three of them were caught in a blizzard. Even Leon looked tickled to see the elephant playing with such delight.

*

That night Will dreamed his mother was alive and he was home again, the two of them sitting in their doorway drinking raspberry leaf tea sweetened with honey. It made him so happy that he tried to stay with the dream, squeezing his eyelids shut, but he couldn't hold onto it. He kept rising to the surface of the morning, and his life as it was now.

After breakfast, Leon hitched up the horse to make deliveries. Toong had to be chained in the aisle while Will mucked out her stall. As he pushed the loaded wheelbarrow toward the outside door, the elephant squealed for her breakfast.

"Hold on," Will called over his shoulder, "I'm almost finished."

There was a rumbling in Toong's belly. Left to herself, the elephant stretched her trunk, searching the ground for spilled grain. Then, investigating the rafters, she came across Leon's jug. With a gurgle of pleasure, Toong pulled the cork and swallowed the entire gallon of rum.

Minutes later, Leon came looking for Will. The elephant's tail stiffened. One look at those flapping ears, that trunk stretched out like a ramrod, and Leon backed out the door.

Will was returning with the wheelbarrow when the elephant bellowed. He saw Leon run out of the barn, then scramble up the embankment as though all his rheumatism had gone.

"What's happening?" the boy called, but the handyman didn't stop. Will watched him disappear around the corner of the building.

Then Will heard a bawl, the likes of which he'd never heard before. "Toong!" he shouted, dropping the wheelbarrow. Something horrible must be going on — the barn door was flapping open. Will ran inside to the elephant. There she was, still chained where he had left her.

When she screamed this time, Will had to cover his ears against the blast. "Toong, Toong," he pleaded, trying to calm her. "What's wrong?"

The elephant seemed to fill the entire space with her restless thrashing. Her front foot began to swing viciously at the packed earth and her eyes blazed with anger. Her legs were chained, one leg to another, and they were fastened on either side to stout poles that supported the roof. Will watched with horror as Toong strained against the poles. He feared that, like Samson, she would pull the pillars down upon their heads.

Suddenly, with a series of snaps, the chains gave way. Will backed into the stall as the elephant broke out of the barn, bursting open the wide doors.

"Godfrey!" he exclaimed. Will ran out in time to see Toong crash through the fence rails and barrel down the path to the road. She stopped once to announce herself in clarion tones. Then she disappeared around the far side of the store.

The boy stood there, helpless. What had set her off?

Leon had taken refuge in the loft. Badly shaken, he climbed down from above. His hands trembled and his foot slipped on the ladder. "Infernal creature," he was ranting. "I'm gettin' rid of it if no one else will."

This alarmed Will. The old man was always making threats, but this time he sounded as if he meant it.

The boy sniffed. There was something familiar about that smell. Then he spied the overturned jug. Rum. Now and then during the day, Will caught the handyman taking a nip. "To oil my joints," Leon would say.

Will held up the jug. "She got into your likker," he said. "She's drunk, that's what she is. I'd better tell Sanderson."

Will started to run. He tripped once and picked himself up. Taking Leon's shortcut, he climbed up the embankment to the store, slipping on the wet grass, and ran through the back entrance. The storeroom was empty.

Mrs. Sanderson was out front, talking while she measured some trimming for a customer.

Will burst in. "Where's Mr. Sanderson."

"Upstairs." Suspicion narrowed Mrs. Sanderson's eyes. "What's goin' on."

Will didn't stop to explain. "Elephant's out," he yelled, pounding up the back stairs.

Loafers, warming themselves at the fire, rushed outside

for a look. "I told you this would happen, didn't I?" Mrs. Sanderson said, throwing up her hands. But nobody was listening.

Will flung open the door at the top of the stairs. "Mr. Sanderson!"

The storekeeper was enveloped in steam, making a poultice for an ailing cow. He turned, still stirring the mess over the fire.

"The elephant . . ." Will was breathing hard. "She broke out."

Sanderson dropped the spoon. "Where's she now?"

"Out on the road, I think," said Will, as the storekeeper snatched his jacket from a peg near the door. "She got into some likker." Sanderson ran back to take the kettle off the fire. ". . . but it ain't her fault," Will tried to explain.

The slop bucket caught his eye. It was full of vegetable peelings from last night's soup. Potato skins were among Toong's favorites. As the storekeeper clattered down the stairs, Will grabbed the bucket. An apple and a carrot lay in the bottom of the dry sink. He threw them in, for good measure.

Leon was waiting in the delivery wagon next to the store. He pointed to tracks in the mud as Will and Mr. Sanderson climbed aboard. "Looks ta me like she's headed toward Chilmark," he said. Will caught his breath when he saw the musket under Leon's seat.

Across the road, George Peebles and two of his cronies

were struggling with Betsy. The frightened horse had over-turned her cart in a ditch, but Leon didn't stop to help. He turned Nell's head and started off at a good clip.

"Elmer's comin'," George shouted after them. "He's gone to get his gun."

Will scanned the fields for Toong. Every pile of stones and distant woodlot seemed to be harboring an elephant shape. He wouldn't let Leon shoot her, but someone else might get her first.

The little Goff boy stood in his family's pasture with a flock of sheep. He shouted something as they went by but they couldn't make out what it was. He was pointing in the direction they were heading. Sure enough, there were fresh droppings in the road. Toong had been this way. But what would they do when they caught up with her?

It was Will who spotted the elephant just over the town line. "There she is!" he pointed. " — behind the Nortons' house!"

Toong was in the Nortons' kitchen garden, snapping off the last row of kale.

Leon pulled in Nell while they were still some distance away. Like George Peeble's Betsy, she might shy at the elephant and they didn't want another runaway.

Will turned at the sound of a second wagon. It was George with a wagonload of men, and behind him, Elmer Athearn. Elmer was riding bareback, a musket under his elbow.

"Please," Will begged, clutching Sanderson's sleeve. "Keep them off. Let me try first." Picking up a length of rope from the floor of the wagon, he clambered down with his bucket.

Cautiously, Will approached Toong. Frightened faces were watching at one of the Nortons' windows. At first the elephant didn't notice Will, her eyesight wasn't all that good. She had polished off the kale and now she was nosing around in a thick hay mulch, uncovering some parsley that hadn't frozen.

Toong pulled up a bunch of the parsely, knocking the dirt off against her knees. Her ears pricked as Will got closer. Then she extended her trunk to catch his scent.

Will kept a hundred feet or so between himself and the elephant. He was afraid of spooking her if he came closer. Moving slowly, he took the apple out of the bucket and tossed it half the distance. Her ears flapped and she eyed it warily.

Even though the day was raw, sweat soaked the back of Will's shirt. He wasn't sure how the elephant would react toward him. Sanderson and the other men had climbed down in readiness, Leon and Elmer with their guns raised. When Toong saw them, she began to swing her head from side to side. Then she lifted her trunk and bellowed.

Vexed, Will motioned the men to stay where they were. They would spoil everything. Slowly he advanced to the apple and rolled it closer. Then he waited. In the silence, he could hear the elephant blowing. She swayed slightly, as if she were making up her mind, but she didn't go for it. Will sighed. Maybe this wasn't going to work.

Walking backward, he began to retreat, leaving a trail of scraps — potato peelings, carrot tops, and shreds of wilted cabbage — as far as they would lead toward the road. When only the carrot was left in the bucket, he turned his back on Toong and slowly walked away. He didn't think his plan was working until he looked at the men watching. The strain had left their faces. Sanderson was actually grinning.

Will turned his back and stole a peek. Toong had already eaten the apple and was heading down the line of vegetable leavings, delicately picking each one up with the tab on the end of her trunk and sticking it into her mouth.

When the elephant had cleaned up every bit, Will held up the big carrot so she would see it. He broke it into two pieces, dropped them back into the bucket and rattled the chunks. Within seconds, the elephant's long trunk was reaching into the pail.

To the astonishment of everyone there, Toong allowed Will to tie the rope to her harness. "It's been an exciting morning, hasn't it," he crooned to the elephant. "Are you ready to go home?" Toong searched the bucket and his pockets for more tidbits.

Will led the elephant to the road. The men put down their guns, but he saw how they backed away as Toong came closer. Will pulled himself proudly tall. He'd been afraid, too, but *he* was the one who had captured her. For years to come, he knew, the tale would be told in Sanderson's how Will Sleeper, when only a boy, had caught a rampaging elephant.

The door of the Nortons' house opened, and Mr. Norton came out. Ever the businessman, Sanderson went to settle with him. He didn't want to lose customers over any damages. Indeed, it could have been much worse.

Will walked the elephant home as quickly as he could, worrying that she would catch cold. He hovered over Toong as she slept most of the day, but after the long nap she was fit as a fiddle.

Leon wouldn't go near her, even though Will swore she was sober now. The old man was crabby for the rest of the evening. He had lost a good jug of rum as well as a chance to get rid of that infernal beast. But Will felt even closer to the elephant. From now on, he knew, they could trust one another.

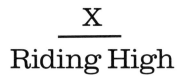

X

Riding High

Spring rain turned the pastures green. At last it was warm enough to keep the elephant outside during the day. Will helped Leon build a pen to hold her, driving the cedar poles deep into the ground. For good measure, they hobbled her legs with stout chain in case she broke out. Toong ate every bit of new green that poked up through the ground, and out of boredom, she rooted up pebbles to throw at the house. When Will brought her in at night, he checked her mouth for concealed ammunition. Two of the barn windows had already been broken.

One hot afternoon, Will took the elephant to bathe in Sheriff's Pond. It was a secluded spot, tucked between two hills behind the store. Raising her trunk, Toong smelled the water even before she saw it. She quickened her pace over the rise and down the grassy bank to the pond so that Will had to run to keep up. When they reached the edge of the pond he dropped the lead rope. Toong waded in and showered water over her back.

The sun on the ripples was dazzling and the opposite bank shimmered with heat. Will sprawled in the grass, watching the elephant's dull, wrinkled skin turn dark and glistening. Then she sank down blissfully and rolled, stirring the water into a muddy soup topped with yellow foam.

Will lay back and looked up at the sky. A red-tailed hawk whistled, rising above him on the updrafts. Then, with a stab of worry, he remembered Peacock. The man would be coming soon to take away the elephant. Will shook his head, driving the thought away. If he didn't think about it maybe it wouldn't happen.

His scalp itched with sweat. He wriggled irritably as an ant scurried across his bare toes and inside a trouser leg. Hauling himself to his feet, he stepped gingerly into the pond, gasping as the chill water crept up to his crotch. Then he took a deep breath and plunged in, flailing his arms a few strokes. Like his grandfather and the other fishermen, he had never learned to swim. They reckoned it was a more merciful death to drown quickly, if their boat sank, then to die of the cold.

Will grabbed for the elephant's tail and she towed him out to deeper water. On impulse, he pulled himself closer to the rough, black island of her back and climbed onto it. He crawled unsteadily up her spine. Once he could grasp her harness, it was easy to sit astride her neck in the warm sun.

The lily pads rustled against the elephant's sides as she waded to shore and began to climb out. One big shoulder, then the other, rose and dropped, each step thrusting Will higher in the air. He had to cling like a tick to keep his balance. But on level ground it was easier: Toong's gait was like the bobbing of a dory in fine weather.

On her own, she headed for home, reaching up to snap off the young branches as they passed by Sanderson's orchard. Who had trained her, Will wondered. Someone long ago? She seemed used to bearing a rider. Will looked down on the elephant's broad forehead and wished he could know the other memories secreted there. He was jealous that she might have been fond of another master. What other commands had he taught her?

The cold water had refreshed Will, and the bright sun and the puffy clouds matched his mood as he rode high above the young cedar trees that dotted the pasture. If only someone could see him now.

"Hey! Look at me," Will crowed as Leon came out of the barn.

"Take care now!" the man scolded. "You'll be breakin' your neck. How're you fixin' to get down?"

Will looked around. He hadn't thought about that. There was no way to guide the elephant, no reins, no stirrups. And it was a long way to the ground.

"Watch out!" Leon warned. It was feeding time. Toong was making tracks for the open door.

"Stop her, quick!" Will yelled as her pace quickened. But it was too late.

Will threw his leg over and jumped, just as the elephant's head ducked under the door frame.

Leon broke his fall. "Tarnation," the old man grumbled, getting to his feet. "I told ya to be careful."

But even Leon's sourness could not spoil Will's feeling of triumph. After he had fed Toong he went to tell the Sandersons about his ride. It was near closing time and the storekeeper was counting what cash there was in the drawer.

"Here he is now," Lottie said.

"We was just talkin' about you," said the storekeeper.

"What about school?" Mrs. Sanderson asked Will. "The summer term'll be startin' the end of the month."

Will shook his head. "Only little kids go to school in the summer," he told her. "I read good already, and I can do sums. Besides, there's too much to do, takin' care of the elephant."

"Don't see that Peacock feller yet," she said, looking pointedly at her husband. "It's already June."

Sanderson sighed and locked the drawer, but Mrs. Sanderson hadn't finished her say. "Mark me." She tapped a finger on the counter with each word. "That man ain't showin' up." And she gave the wood one last rap with her knuckles.

The possibility made Will feel hopeful. He shut his eyes.

Oh please don't let him come, he prayed under his breath. I'll be so good!

*

Riding Toong back from the pond was just the beginning. Since Peacock had taught the elephant to bow, Will got her to kneel down all the way so that he could climb on and off. And he discovered he could steer Toong like a horse, pushing behind her ears with his toes. From then on he rode the elephant every day to give her exercise, roaming the pastures and quiet ways and avoiding the public roads.

One bright afternoon they ventured as far as Tiah's Cove Road. Will's excitement grew as the elephant shuffled down the familiar lane. He often thought about living here on his own. He could do it; he knew he could. The days when his mother was sick, he had taken care of everything and he didn't need much.

Something swelled large in Will's chest at the sight of the house. The roof sagged at a new angle and the place seemed smaller. It looked sad now as if all the life had gone out of it. He got down and tied the elephant.

Someone had put a lock on the door. Shading his eyes, Will pressed his face against the window. Everything was still there. His mother's bed stood in the middle of the room. It wouldn't be the same here without her. When Will thought about this house he remembered all the good times he and Maddy had had living here. But the stripped bed with its stained mattress brought back to him the last desperate weeks of her sickness.

Inside, below the window, a small bird lay stiff and unnatural on the floor. Its beady eye stared. It must have battered itself trying to get out. Will stepped back. All he saw now was his reflection and the elephant's. Will untied Toong and led her away, sorry now that he had come back here.

Before the house was out of sight, he stopped for one last look. Just then he heard voices. Will turned. Peter, Walter, and Wood Tick were at the end of the lane. Will stopped, but it was too late. They had seen him.

"What'er ya doin'?" Walter asked when Will came abreast of them.

"Walkin'," he muttered, not looking at any of them. He was in no mood for their games.

Peter yanked up a clump of dandelions and waved them in front of the elephant.

"Leave her alone," Will said.

"You're not the boss. I can do what I want. Here. Here ya go." Peter held out the weeds, teasing the elephant and then pulling them away.

"Come on, Toong," Will said, yanking at her rope.

The elephant towered over them. Lifting her trunk, she squealed. Then she scooped up a trunkful of dirt and showered it over the boys.

Peter let out a howl and stumbled into his friends as they backed away.

Will bit his lip, trying not to laugh. Toong did this all the time, sometimes when the flies were biting, and sometimes just because she found a nice pile of dust. Picking up a dead branch he poked her leg. "Toong, down!" he commanded, and from a safe distance, the three other boys watched bug-eyed as Toong sank to her knees.

Will clambered on as smoothly as he could and grabbed the elephant's head band. "Toong, hup. Hup!" he said, and the elephant got to her feet. As yet he couldn't count on her moving when he wanted her to, but sooner or later she would get going. This time she started toward the three boys at a good trot. It was getting near suppertime, and she looked forward to her ration of grain.

Peter and his friends had been standing transfixed. As the elephant bore down on them, they whooped and scattered, scrambling between the fence rails to get away. When at last Toong slowed to a walk, Will looked back. All he could see of the boys were three lines of trampled grass.

XI

Losing Toong

The stranger arrived late in June. Will was cleaning the store, dusting jars and boxes and replacing them on the shelves. The little man walked in and handed Sanderson a letter. His clothes, a coat split in the tail like a barn swallow and a tall stovepipe of a hat, weren't like anything Will had seen before.

"You are this person?" the man asked Sanderson, pointing to the storekeeper's name on the envelope.

"Yessir. What can I do for you?"

"Franzini," the man said, pointing to a place on the document and then at his own chest. "That's me." He reminded Will of the small but ferocious banty rooster his mother once had.

Because of the man's rapid, broken speech, Will barely understood what he was saying. Maybe Sanderson was having trouble with it, too, because, while Franzini talked on about the roads between here and Providence and how his wagon had broken an axle, the storekeeper was puzzling out the letter Franzini had given to him. At the mention of Providence, Will listened more closely. Peacock had gone to Providence.

When Sanderson finished reading, he looked at the man over the tops of his glasses. "So," he said, folding the letter. "You came to take the elephant." The storekeeper spoke very loudly as if the foreign man was hard of hearing.

"Yes, yes." Franzini wiped his face with a large handkerchief. "Is my elephant, now. I pay for it."

Will's heart began to beat faster. He couldn't believe this was really happening.

The visitor spread his hands. "I tour whole country. Walk rope." To demonstrate, he held out his arms as if to balance himself. "Now I go to Boston and take elephant with me."

Sanderson smiled and bobbed his head. "Well, fine. Take her any time you want."

No — Will wanted to protest. No, you can't do that. Instead, his throat was choked with rage toward both of them, the storekeeper and this man who was taking his elephant.

Unaware of the boy who was crouched behind the flour barrel, the little man went on. "All night I travel with my partner. Now we sleep in loft."

"Sure, sure. Go right ahead." Sanderson took the man's elbow and led him out the back way to the barn.

Will leaned his forehead against the barrel and shut his eyes. He had spent so much time with the elephant. It didn't seem fair that a stranger could just walk and in and take her away.

A short while later Mrs. Sanderson came downstairs. She stopped and pulled back her chin at Will's gloomy look. "You got the stomach ache?" she asked, frowning.

"The elephant's goin' away," Will growled, knowing how happy this news would make her.

Mrs. Sanderson looked around, surprised. "You mean Peacock is here?"

Will barely shook his head. "Some other man."

The back door banged as Sanderson came in. "See this?" He waved a bank draft at Mrs. Sanderson. "I told you thing would turn out all right. This will pay for what we've spent on the elephant . . . and with a nice profit."

Mrs. Sanderson squinted carefully at the bank check. She wasn't convinced that easily.

But Sanderson was in high spirits. "This foreign feller's buying her," Sanderson explained. ". . . Some kinda travelin' performer. Has a woman with him, and they're takin' the elephant to Boston."

With a grim set to his mouth, Will went back to cleaning the shelves. He resented how glad the Sandersons were to be rid of the elephant. Likely, they wouldn't mind being

free of him, too, he thought, scrubbing at a sticky ring of molasses.

Later, when the store became oppressively hot, Will left to bathe the elephant. A blue cart with a canvas shelter stood next to the barn. The word FRANZINI was painted on its side in curliques and gold letters and a sign was nailed to it.

The barnyard baked in the hot sun. Toong had thrown dirt over her back to protect her skin and she stood dusty and forlorn, waiting for Will. "You won't be penned up much longer," he said, scratching her trunk. "You'll be glad to get out of here, won't you."

The elephant looked wise and patient. Will unchained her and led her over to the gate. If only they could run away together, he and Toong, and never come back to Cadbury.

Will stopped a moment and thought about it. Why not? Now that the trees were leafed out, it would cost nothing to feed the elephant on the road. He pictured the two of them roaming the countryside. When they were far enough away they would sleep in the woods till it was dark. They could travel at night like Peacock had, stopping in small towns where people would pay to see Toong. Soon he would have enough money to buy his own wagon.

Will climbed up on her back and they started across the pasture. The grass was long and lush, alive with grasshoppers springing ahead of the elephant's feet. He felt jubilant. Soon the two of them would be free. "No more pen," he murmured to Toong's ear. "And no more work for me."

Toong headed at a trot for their pond. Wading knee deep, she showered them both. "Hey!" Will called as cold water soaked into his clothing. Dark trickles ran down the elephant's dusty skin and she sank to her knees. He slid down her shoulder into the water. Picking up a handful of dirt from the sandy botton, he scrubbed her, laughing as she rolled slightly and squeezed her eyes shut.

But later, when Will lay on the bank watching the elephant bathe, he realized his plan was hopeless. He couldn't hide her for very long. Franzini would come after them and take her away. People had been jailed for stealing a sheep and Toong was much more valuable.

The elephant had hollowed a cool spot for herself in the mud. Unconcerned, she lay sprawled in her wallow. She didn't care about anything, Will thought to himself, as long as she got her food and her bath. It hurt him to think she could be happy with her new owner.

The shadows of afternoon lengthened across the water. Will squinted over the treetops at the position of the sun. He had to get back — the Sandersons wanted him to finish cleaning the shelves. He rolled over with a groan. Why was he angry with them, he wondered. *They* hadn't sold the elephant. But, somehow, he felt they had let him down.

Will washed off the elephant and they started back. A woman was waiting on the seat of the blue cart, a bonnet shading her from the sun, and Franzini was pacing the yard. "Toong. Down." Will tapped the elephant with a stick. Aware of the man's eyes on him, he spoke louder to her than necessary.

Toong sank to her knees and Will slid off, trying hard to land on his feet and not his bottom. Up close, he saw that the acrobat's face was seamed with many lines. A scar ran across the bridge of his nose. "I go now," Franzini said, taking a rope from the back of the wagon.

"But I haven't showed you what she needs," Will said, shocked by the man's haste. ". . . how to take care of her."

Franzini dismissed him with a wave of his hand. "Peacock tell me everything already."

Will's concern grew into panic. This was happening too fast for him. He turned to the woman, hoping for an ally, but she looked away. Her face was hidden by the bonnet.

Will turned back to the acrobat. "Take me with you," he said on impulse. "You see she obeys me good."

Franzini shook his head. Tossing the rope around the elephant's neck, he caught the other end. With a squeal of surprise, Toong rose to her feet. But the man moved like lightning and whipped the rope into a knot.

Will swallowed hard. Surely Toong would refuse to follow. But obedient as a pet lamb, she let herself be led to the wagon. Will felt as though she had betrayed him.

But the boy persisted. "It's a lot of work," he argued. "You've got to brush her every day. You've got to feed her. She eats a *lot*."

"I take care of it," Franzini said, tying the elephant to the wagon.

". . . and water. She drinks gallons of it!"

The cart horse, a bony gray, shifted restlessly. Unused to the presence of the elephant, he bobbed his head, rattling the traces. The woman braced both hands on either side of the seat to steady herself.

Will grabbed the man's sleeve. "I could take care of your horse, too, a-a-and . . ."

"*Basta*," the man yelled to quiet the horse. Brushing Will aside, he climbed in the cart. "Don't need anyone," were his last words.

With a click to the horse and a clatter of wheels, he was off. "*Please*," Will begged, running alongside. "You don't even have to pay me." But Franzini didn't stop.

Will stood in the wheel tracks fighting back tears until he saw the last of the cart and the elephant shuffling behind it. Then he stamped his foot, feeling helpless and angry.

Trudging back to the barn, he saw Leon watching him. Will's face grew hot with shame. Had Leon seen him pleading with the foreigner? Will swiped at his wet cheeks, streaking them with his grimy hands.

He walked over to the pump and worked the handle vigorously, splashing his face with cold water. He didn't want any of them seeing him cry, least of all Leon. Then, marching past the old man, Will started cleaning Toong's stall, furiously shoveling dirt in the grooves her feet had worn, and tamping them smooth with a rake. By milking time, he had removed every sign of the elephant from the barn. But he couldn't erase her lumpy, sagging form from his mind.

Nothing was said about the work Will left unfinished in the store, and to his relief, there was no mention of the elephant at supper. There was never much talk anyway once Mrs. Sanderson put food on the table.

That night Will missed the familiar sound of the elephant in the next stall. The barn seemed unusually bright without her bulk in front of the window, blocking out the moonlight.

He had lost everyone, Grandfather and Mother, and the father he had never seen. And now he had lost Toong. He hadn't said good-bye to any of them; they had all been taken too soon for that. But Toong hadn't died. She was out there somewhere.

Sleepless, Will lay thinking of their last ride together and how she had enjoyed rolling in the mud. He was sorry now that he'd resented her for being happy. Some day when he grew up, he would set out to find her and buy her back. Would she know him by then, he wondered? He hoped elephants lived for a long time like horses.

Then he had a terrible thought. What if he was too late? Suppose Franzini didn't look after her right. Will thought of her walking all day in the hot sun. Did this man know how sensitive she was? Franzini was an acrobat. What did *he* know about elephants. Suppose she got sick? Franzini only wanted Toong in order to make money. He didn't really care about her the way Will did. He might even be cruel to her.

Will imagined a curious crowd of people gathered to stare at Toong. In his mind he saw the elephant thin and haggard, too weak to stand up. Her suffering eyes searched the crowd for him. She didn't understand why he wasn't there.

Will sat up. He couldn't wait for years to find her again. Tomorrow he would catch up with Franzini. He and the elephant could not be separated.

*

Will was up early the next morning. Before the first customer came in, he had washed the last of the shelves and dumped the soapy water in the lilac bushes.

Mrs. Sanderson was working at a desk in the back room, adding a long column of figures. Will set down the empty bucket and stood there nervously until she looked up.

"I'm leaving," he said.

That was the hardest part. After that the rest tumbled out. "I'm going after them . . . after the elephant."

Mrs. Sanderson was taken aback. "That don't make no sense, Will. You got a good place right here."

Will expected she would say something like that.

"Who knows what trouble you'll run into," she said. "You've never been nowheres before."

Will couldn't let himself think about those things.

"You don't even know as you'll find 'em," Mrs. Sanderson added.

"I'll find 'em," he said stubbornly. "That's all."

Mrs. Sanderson pursed her lips. For once, she had nothing more to say.

Will fixed his eyes on the desk top. "I-I just wanted you to know" — he rubbed his fingertips along the smoothworn edge of the wood — "that I'm grateful to ya."

Mrs. Sanderson removed her glasses and set them down carefully. Then she braced her arms on the desktop and considered for a while. Will waited, feeling uncomfortable.

Finally, he heard a sigh. "Well then," Mrs. Sanderson said, snapping shut her account book. "If you're bound to do it there's no stoppin' you, I guess." She stood, pushing herself up with a small grunt. Her knees had stiffened from sitting and she tottered slightly on her way out to the counter.

"I'm not lettin' you go off scattered. You gotta take somethin' to eat." Mrs. Sanderson whacked a chunk from a wheel of yellow cheese and wrapped it in brown paper along with a loaf of bread.

"What about shoes?" she challenged. "Ain't you takin' no shoes?"

Will looked down at his bare feet. He had outgrown the boots they had given him. "No, Ma'am." He curled his toes. "I like walkin' this way."

Mrs. Sanderson's mouth worked as she looked at him

for a long moment. Will squirmed under her gaze. "You had better say good-bye to the Mister," she said at last.

Will lowered his eyes. "Yes'm."

"Remember . . ." Will was surprised when her voice faltered. "You can always come back," she said.

At that moment Will wasn't at all sure he was doing the right thing.

XII

Along the Road

The sun was setting when the cart hung with churns and kettles stopped at a crossroad. Will jumped down from the seat and thanked the peddlar.

"Just keep on this road headin' north," the man said, handing down Will's pack. "Sooner or later you'll get to Boston." He looked down at the boy and shook his head. "It's a long ways from here, lad."

For a moment Will felt doubtful about finding the elephant. Maybe he should go home. He pictured how it would be returning to Cadbury, sleeping again in Leon's room and working in the store. No, he thought, I can't go back. Besides, Franzini had gotten less than a day's start — Will would catch up with him soon. Before he turned down the unfamiliar road, he forced himself to smile at the man and wave him on.

The road wound gradually uphill. At the top of a rise Will caught his breath. Only a spark of light here and there told him of a farmhouse in the distance.

Then the fields were swallowed by forest. Once he entered its shadow, the chorus of insects ended and even the stars were hidden. Will stumbled along, lurching into holes and sliding on the loose stones. His right hand was raised protectively as if any moment he would collide with the solid wall of darkness.

Frogs peeped: The din grew almost deafening. There must be a swamp nearby, he thought. Gradually, the sound faded. Over his shoulder he saw a pair of glinting green lights. Eyes were watching him — a raccoon or a deer, maybe.

Will's head turned when a twig snapped. "Please, let it be morning soon," he prayed.

Will felt a hard lump in his pocket, the two silver dollars. He tried to recall the storekeeper's words on the porch that morning. Mr. Sanderson had motioned him to sit down and he listened while Will confessed that he was going away.

Sanderson had leaned toward him and put his freckled hand over Will's. Will remembered just how the hand had felt, hard and dry.

"You know . . ." The storekeeper paused. "Leon isn't going to be much use soon and we'll have to take on someone else. A hard working boy, one who's determined like you . . . no telling what he could do for himself right here."

Will didn't know how to answer. He wasn't prepared for this reaction from Sanderson. He had thought that maybe the man would be angry.

Finally Sanderson broke the silence. "Is that what's most important to you?" Sanderson asked. "The elephant?"

Will admitted it was.

The storekeeper had shrugged and opened his hands expansively. "Then go after her. Why sure!" Will had felt such great relief that he broke out in a smile.

Sanderson had gone inside. Taking two silver dollars from the cash drawer, he knotted them in a brand-new handkerchief. "Here," he said. "This is for you. Everyone needs a little start."

Will fingered the handkerchief in his pocket. "You're a lucky boy," Sanderson had told him, "to know what you're after." Plodding on, he lost all sense of time passing as he followed the pale ribbon of road. Soon, he thought to himself, the sky would lighten. If he could only hold out.

When Will emerged from the forest, he saw the outline of hills. From trees and hedgerows the first sleepy birds called. He had made it through the night.

At the end of a lane bordered by huge maple trees, smoke rose from the chimney of a farmhouse. Right now the family would be sitting down to a hearty breakfast. Will felt a gnawing ache in his stomach. He sat down and ate some of his cheese and bread.

A brook ran under the road. Will climbed down and drank from it, wiping his mouth on the back of his sleeve. The milky sky was turning clear and blue. It was going to be hot today. On trembling legs, Will followed the down-hill road as far as the entrance to the lane and collapsed in the shade. Folding his jacket under his head, he fell asleep at once.

*

Something was buzzing. Will opened one eye, looking sleepily around him. Next to his ear, a bee probed a nodding pink clover. A root poked painfully into his back and he shifted. It must be midmorning. The sun had worked its way up the sky already and it was warm. His hair and his clothing were damp with sweat.

Will got painfully to his feet. He was thirsty again. As he bent to pick up the pack his head throbbed from the heat and he staggered to keep his balance.

He felt better after he washed his face and drank more of the cool water. The fields spread out below him, their patchwork blurred by the shimmering heat. Will caught his breath. Working its way along the valley was a cart, from this distance as small as a child's toy. And tied behind it was the unmistakable shape of the elephant plodding along.

Will was ready to plunge after them, straight down through the fields and woods; but in the long run he knew, it would take less time to follow the road. Somewhere it must connect with the valley. Will started off at a jog-trot, full of excitement and hope. The road was hot and he was limping from the large blisters on the bottom of each foot, but he couldn't lose them now.

The blood pounded in his head. It was a relief when the road led into the shade of a woodlot, but here clouds of stinging black flies danced in front of his eyes. Frantically, Will scratched his back and waved his arms. Then he snapped off a large fern to fan away the flies. A maddening bite throbbed at his temple, swelling one of his eyelids shut. Finally in spite of the heat, he had to put on his jacket, turning up the collar before the insects ate him alive.

Leaves rustled as a sudden breeze cooled his skin. He looked up to see dark clouds moving across the strip of sky. Will heard the first big drops fall on the leaves over-head, then they hit the dust ahead of his feet. Suddenly rain beat down, raising up a fine mist with the smell of earth on it. He ran for shelter under a tree but soon the leaves bent under their burden, soaking him.

Will was anxious now that the cart was out of sight. He pushed the dripping hair out of his eyes and started walking again. At least the mud felt soothing to his burning feet. He broke off a dead branch for a walking stick, bracing himself as he skittered down the slippery hill. He had to catch sight of the cart again before dark.

*

The sign on the road marker said WHAREHAM. Will stopped and looked where it pointed to the left. Here the houses crowded close together, unlike the scattered farms in Cadbury. Surely, Will thought, if the wagon came this way someone has seen the elephant.

The rain had ended and above the trees the summer haze was stained with a rosy glow as if the village were on fire. Soon it would be dark. Will backed off the road as a large farm wagon rattled around the bend, heading toward the town. Noisy children hung over the sides shouting, "Go home, Cap," to the bony hound that was following them.

The creature veered toward Will, its tongue lolling. Will clutched his bundle higher, but the hound only sniffed at his trousers and then hurried on.

The main street through Whareham was filled with people, their faces lit by pine torches set out in front of a tavern. Music was playing, and overhead the trees shook with boys who had climbed up for a better look. Will felt the excitement of something about to happen. A row of handbills fluttered from the fence on either side of the tavern and he pushed forward to read them.

Loud barks exploded in his ear. A big shepherd dog lunged toward him from the back of a wagon, its bared teeth close to his face. It barked again at the hound running loose. Shrinking back Will saw, to his relief, that the shepherd was tied. Still, his heart pounded.

Two little girls bumped against him. They giggled shyly, and went back to chasing each other around their mothers' skirts. Will's attention was drawn to the tavern porch where a slender musician was playing on a silver pipe. The boy drew closer. He had heard musical instruments before but he had never seen a fantastical costume like the one this person wore. It was made of a shiny stuff, one side red, the other white. A mask hid the player's eyes, and his tall hat split into two tails hung with bells and tassels. Will leaned his elbows on the porch and listened. Before long, he was swaying to the tune.

The eyes behind the piper's mask were watching him. Will could see their glitter. Then the most thrilling thing happened. The musician stopped and beckoned him to come up. Will hesitated. The piper smiled and beckoned again, more insistently this time.

Will couldn't say no. He pulled himself up onto the porch. From the street Will had thought the fellow bigger, but now standing next to him, he saw they were nearly the same height. A drum hung from the piper's neck and it hampered his movement as he hopped about. The fellow lifted the strap from his own neck and hung it around Will's. Then he placed felt-covered sticks in the boy's hands.

Will panicked. Not in front of all these people! "I don't know how to play," he said.

"Then this will be your first time." The voice startled Will. The piper was a woman!

"It's easy." The piper sounded so positive that, again, he couldn't refuse. She stood behind Will to show him, swinging his arm below the elbow in a circle, hitting the drum alternately with each swing.

BOOM BOOM, BOOM BOOM. It was a powerful sound.

"Don't stop," she said.

The piper picked up a tune to follow his rhythm. Will knew the tune, it was an old chantey his mother used to sing. At first he was too frightened to do anything but move his arms as the musician had moved them. BOOM BOOM. But the time seemed to drag a little so he speeded it up, even though the rest of him felt frozen with embarrassment, especially his face.

Keeping pace with him, the pipe became more sprightly and the piper turned and nodded her approval at Will. This put the boy more at ease. He was even able to look over the crowd. Never had so many eyes been on him since Toong had found the gingerbread in his pocket. He had been so afraid of the elephant then. Where was she now?

The drum was getting heavy. The strap pressed on his neck and his arms were tired, but he steeled himself to the discomfort.

"Stop!"

The piper had spoken.

With great relief, Will leaned over and rested the drum on the floor, pulling the strap over his head.

The tavern door had been wide open. Now that the music stopped, the men inside spilled out onto the wide porch, arguing about crops and politics. One of them raised his arm and pointed to the high, two-story building across the street. "Look," he shouted. "Someone's on Gifford's roof."

A ripple of astonishment spread through the crowd. Two points of fire had burst into flames above the peak of the roof. Between them stood a man holding a long rod with burning pitch on each end, his white shirt and face lit by the fire. Will recognized the compact figure at once. It was Franzini. A rope stretched from around the chimney where the man stood, all the way across the broad street to the tavern roof.

As the crowd watched, Franzini stepped up on the rope and balanced briefly on one foot. It trembled so that even Will could see the rope vibrate. Then Franzini set his other foot ahead of the first. Slowly he inched out over the road, using the burning rod for balance.

The mood of the crowd had changed. It was no longer restless and joking. Indeed, the only sound was the hiss of burning pitch. Will hung over the porch rail, intent on every step the man took. He jumped when a torch near him suddenly flared.

Franzini began walking faster, so rapidly that the full sleeves of his shirt fluttered. He had almost reached the other side when he stopped. Turning carefully, he started back. Will was confused. Why would the man go back when he was almost safe? The ropewalker paused over the center of the road. Poised on the balls of his feet, he bowed and the crowd applauded.

A loud gasp went up. The applause was cut short. Franzini had lost his balance.

His stick whipped the air, writing arcs of flame against the sky. A woman screamed. Franzini was falling.

From then on it all happened so fast that it was hard for Will to follow it. The rope caught Franzini under the legs, and on the upward bounce he stood again. Nimbly and effortlessly, he ran to the safety of the chimney.

The crowd cheered the Great Franzini and he answered them with a second bow. Then, in another amazing move, he walked along the ridgepole and stepped out into what looked like thin air, sliding down a rope attached to a stake in the ground. He slid so rapidly that some insisted they saw a trail of smoke behind him.

Will was stunned, reliving what had happened in his mind. Suddenly it dawned on him — the ropewalker had fallen on purpose. Will felt foolish at having been tricked, and a little resentful because of it, but still he had to admire this man. Spellbound, he had forgotten the elephant for a short while. What had Franzini done with her?

Next to him the piper pulled off her mask and hat. Shaking loose a cloud of red hair, she jumped down into the audience. A shock went through Will. "Mother!" he cried after her.

XIII

A Light in the Darkness

It was like one of his nightmares. Will knew his mother was dead. He had even gone back home again to be sure. But there she was: he had seen her with his own eyes.

With hope rising, Will climbed down after the woman, pushing his way between the people who were milling around. "Mother! Mother, come back," he cried, but she slipped behind a wagon and the crowd seemed to swallow her up. In their holiday mood, the people around him were laughing and talking, unaware of his desperation.

Will caught a glimpse of the woman's red and white costume, bright against the drab farm clothes of the others. He struggled to keep her in sight. This time it wasn't a dream. He mustn't lose her now. At last, he caught up with her. She had stopped to collect donations in her forked hat.

Will clutched at her sleeve. "Mother," he said.

She turned and Will drew back — it was the face of a stranger.

Will was stunned. Tears of disappointment stung his eyes, blurring the woman's face. He blinked them back. "I-I'm . . ." Now he was too upset to speak, but the woman seemed not to have heard him. She snatched off his cap and dropped some coins into it. "Work the other side of the street," she said, shaking the hat so the money would jingle.

Will stood helplessly with the cap between his hands.

"Hurry," the woman said, shoving him into the crowd, ". . . before they all leave."

A few people dropped coins in Will's cap, but he wasn't aware of them. He could see the blue cart now, next to the tavern. It was late and the crowd was dissolving. To hold them longer, Franzini was standing on the seat, spinning tin plates on top of a long stick. Wagons filled with farm folk rattled past him out of town. Those who were left returned to the tavern, shutting the door on the last sounds of talk and laughter.

The woman came over to Will and took the hat from his hands. She was slender like Maddy, with the same white skin and reddish hair.

"Huh!" she said, measuring its lightness. "Such a sorrowful face should bring in more."

Will hung his head.

The woman regarded him. "You *are* the boy from Cadbury," she said. "Are you not?"

Will nodded.

"And you're following us?" Hearing sympathy in her tone, Will looked up into the woman's face. Even in this light he could see that she wasn't pretty like his mother. Her face was almost round, with large and protruding eyes, but they were tender and a very clear blue. It was her eyes that made him trust her.

"Come," she said, putting an arm around his shoulder. "We will see what he says."

Franzini looked down at Will from the cart. "What are you doing here?" he demanded.

Will turned to the woman for help. When she didn't respond, he took a big swallow and answered. "I want to go with you." Torchlight blazed in the man's eyes. Will trembled but he held his ground.

"I already told you," the man said. "No."

"Please. I won't cause you no trouble."

"What is your name?"

"Will," he said, hopefully.

"You go home, Will. I don't want no boy with me."

"But . . . I won't take up any room." Will held up the little bundle of all that was left . . . his clothes and his mother's drawings.

"No." Franzini chopped the air. "I say no! You hear me? I don't want no boy . . ."

Will cut into the man's tirade. "Can't I just see her?" he asked, meaning the elephant. "Has she got water?"

"I give water. I give food." Franzini made an angry sweep with his hand. "Now go home.

"Miranda!" He turned to the woman. "We are leaving."

The woman gave Will a regretful glance. Then she untied the horse and climbed up next to the ropewalker.

Will followed them to a narrow lane where the buildings thinned out. When Franzini stopped at the last house, the woman crawled inside their canvas shelter. Getting down, the ropewalker took a chain from the back of the cart and knocked on the side door of the house. An elderly man came out with a lantern. Will watched the two of them go back to a shed where the old man unlocked the door and Franzini went inside with the lantern.

Will sat down on the front steps across the road and waited. In a short time the acrobat appeared leading the elephant. Will jumped to his feet. He could see by the dejected droop of Toong's ears and the angle of her tail that she was unhappy.

Will wanted to go to her at once, to tell her it was all right, that he was here. He held himself back while Franzini chained the elephant behind the wagon. But when the ropewalker hung the lantern and climbed up to the seat, Will ran into the road.

"Toong!"

Franzini looked stonily ahead as he turned his horse toward the center of town, but when the cart came alongside Will, he flicked the reins. Instantly, the horse jerked up its head. It broke into a swift trot and Will had to jump back from the wheels. As the elephant passed, her eye rolled back toward him and she tested the air for his scent, but the chain tightened around her neck and she followed the pull of the cart.

"Toong!" Will cried again, and his voice echoed down the street. He started to run after her. Just as he caught up with them his foot turned in a wagon rut and he went down. Pain stabbed his ankle. He watched, forlorn, as the distance grew between him and the elephant. What should he do now?

Will rocked back and forth holding the ankle. He thought of the empty stall and his loneliness back in Cadbury. Would he never see Toong again, never know what happened to her?

The store windows were shuttered and the town was dark except for a light here and there in the rear of a building. Will picked himself up and limped after the wagon. Tears filled his eyes at the thought of another night alone, walking in the dark.

The hound had stayed behind after the crowd left and it was poking through some tasty garbage in front of the tavern. Now the dog caught a new scent, something like cow, but more powerful. Will saw the elephant's ears rise in alert as the hound darted into the street. When the dog came snuffling at Toong's heels, she stopped suddenly and bawled, bracing her legs.

The cart jerked to a halt and Franzini was thrown from his seat. At the same time there was a crash inside the shelter. Will heard Miranda scream.

The elephant wheeled around, dragging the cart sideways. Likely, she would overturn it. The horse reared and plunged between its traces, trying to break free. Luckily Franzini knew how to fall. He leaped up at once and grabbed the reins.

The hound was running back and forth, barking at Toong's heels. Will scrambled to his feet, forgetting the pain in his ankle and his fear of the dog. "Git! Git!" he yelled.

Toong's sides were heaving and her trunk curled, ready to strike, but the hound was used to the game of being chased. Before the elephant could attack, it ducked beneath the tavern porch.

Miranda crawled from under the shelter where she had changed into her street clothes, and was clinging to the seat of the cart. "The prod!" Franzini called to her. ". . . the iron hook for the elephant. Get it. Quick!"

Miranda disappeared under the canvas.

Screaming with frustration, the elephant tried to get at the dog. "Toong. Toong!" Will shouted as she began to tear at the porch. Curious faces appeared at the upper tavern windows. "Toong down," Will demanded again and again, but his voice was lost in the uproar.

Franzini took the elephant prod from Miranda. Hooking it in Toong's harness, he tried to hold her back, but the animal was too strong. The prod was torn from his hands. Franzini picked it up again and began beating the elephant's shoulder. When that had no effect he hit her on the side of the skull.

"Stop!" Will yelled, throwing himself on the man.

Taking little notice of them, the elephant swung her head and knocked the two of them to the ground.

Just then, the door to the tavern burst open. Out came the burly innkeeper with an ancient muzzleloader. The elephant eyed this newcomer, switching her trunk back and forth like the tail of an angry cat.

The innkeeper raised his gun.

"Toong!" Will jumped up on the porch between them. "Look, Toong. It's me. It's Will."

A spark of recognition lit the elephant's eyes. She ran her trunk over Will, snuffling his shirt pockets.

"Good girl," Will crooned, stroking her trunk. The porch made him even with her height. He embraced the great head, laying his face against her rough, wrinkled skin.

Franzini got to his feet. "Keep away. Keep away," he said, taking command of the others. He waved back the innkeeper and the small group of half-dressed patrons that hovered behind him. Calmly, with the air of a man who faced danger every day, he picked up his hat and brushed himself off.

The innkeeper stepped out again. "What about my building? Look at the damage done to it."

"What you mean?" The ropewalker drew himself tall. He pointed to the darkness under the porch. "That dog attacked my elephant. Only one in country. Do you know cost if *she* get damaged?"

The innkeeper was breathing heavily but he didn't answer. At this point Toong raised her trunk and let out another bawl. When the innkeeper backed toward the door, Franzini pushed his advantage. "We leave now before she get upset," he said. "Yesterday she destroy whole building."

Will's jaw dropped open. Was this true?

Miranda had been holding the horse's head. Now Franzini signaled her to get onto the cart. The woman looked at Will and then turned to Franzini. The ropewalker's face was an unreadable mask. Miranda's eyes rose to Franzini's in appeal.

Go on, ask him! Will urged silently. Ask him to take me along.

Miranda's lips parted. Will was certain she was about to speak. But, thinking better of it, she gathered up her skirts and climbed aboard.

Will swallowed hard. Once again they were leaving him

behind. He sized up the chains that bound the elephant to the cart. Mentally he tested them against her strength. Together, could he and Toong resist Franzini? Would the elephant obey if Will commanded her to stay?

Toong shifted nervously; her rolling eye checked for the whereabouts of the dog. In her present state, Will wasn't sure he could count on her. He wavered. Toong's back was just a leap away. Once there, he could insist on going along. Would Franzini risk a scene by making him get off?

The ropewalker broke into Will's thoughts. "Go on. Get up there." He motioned Will to mount the elephant.

The boy hesitated. Did this mean Franzini would let him go with them?

"Go ahead!" The ropewalker made an impatient wave with his hand.

Will would hardly let himself believe it. But before Franzini could change his mind, the boy flung himself on Toong's back. He scrambled toward her head and perched behind it.

Franzini picked up Will's bundle from the street. "You better not cost much to feed," he warned, shaking it at the boy.

"No sir! I don't eat hardly nothin' at all." Will felt such elation that he dared a smile. Looking down from the elephant's height, the ropewalker wasn't so intimidating.

Franzini climbed onto the cart and took up the reins. With a final flourish, he touched his hat to the innkeeper and they started off.

The moon rode beside them out of town. It silvered Toong's head and the roofs of the silent houses. Will looked back to the inn where folks were still watching from the porch. Let 'em stare, he thought. In fact, he enjoyed it. Folks would stare in every town from here to Boston and he looked forward to it.

Soon the houses dwindled down to fields lined with trees. The night was heavy with moisture. Toong pulled down a branch, showering Will with droplets, and he laughed, feeling buoyant.

Now the moon slipped behind the clouds. One of the cartwheels chirped in the darkness. Will hummed along with it, a favorite song of his mother's. His eyes were fixed on the single light ahead, the glow of Franzini's lantern.

What Inspired This Story

Will and Maddy, as well as the rest of the characters in this story, never lived except in my imagination. But in the early 1800s a real person, Hakaliah Bailey, bought Old Bet, an African elephant, from a ship's captain for $1,000. Bailey intended to use this elephant for farm work, but she attracted so much attention on the trip home to Somers, New York, that he decided to charge admission to see her. Imagine how amazed people were at their first sight of such an extraordinary animal.

Bailey persuaded farmers along the way to let him show Old Bet in their barns by day, traveling only under the cover of darkness. In the next few years, Bailey made a fortune, walking the elephant from Maine to Virginia. Eventually he added more animals to his menagerie and this is thought to be the beginning of the traveling circus in America.

Old Bet was shot in Alfred, Maine, in 1816 by a farmer named Donald Davies who felt it was sinful for poor people to spend their hard-earned money to see this "wicked beast." In her memory, Bailey built The Elephant Hotel, which is now the Somers Town Hall and Circus Museum. Out front there is still a granite memorial to Old Bet, topped with the gilded figure of an elephant.

— *Carol Carrick*